If I Only Knew

Angela Grant

Published by

 Melrose Books

An Imprint of Melrose Press Limited
St Thomas Place, Ely
Cambridgeshire
CB7 4GG, UK
www.melrosebooks.co.uk

FIRST EDITION

Copyright © Angela Grant 2018

The Author asserts her moral right to
be identified as the author of this work

Cover by Melrose Books

ISBN   **978-1-912640-03-4 Paperback**
     978-1-912640-04-1 ePub
     978-1-912640-05-8 Mobi

Printed and bound in Great Britain by:
Ashford Colour Press Ltd
Unit 600
Fareham Reach
Fareham Road
Gosport
PO13 0FW

*This is for
my wonderful husband and family*

1

My name is Julie Marshal, born 1992, adopted at nine months. My mother died during child birth due to eclampsia, and my so-called father, in name only, as my mother and he were never married, certainly did not want a a baby as they had planned to emigrate to Australia and the idea of going with a newborn was not in his plan. He was a paramedic and had been offered a job near Melbourne and with mother being a pharmacist, there would be no problem with work. Adoption was the only way for him to go. I was just a few months when, by the grace of God, the most wonderful people called Mr and Mrs Marshall adopted me. I was the luckiest baby on earth as they were the most loving and incredible parents you could wish for. I was truly blessed. It wasn't until I was in my early teens that they told me that I had been adopted. But for me they were my parents and not for one moment did I ever have the desire to find my blood father. After all, he didn't want me. Why the hell would I ever want him? As far as I was concerned he did not exist. Both my parents were teachers at the 'Nicolas Academy' where I was educated. My father was Deputy Head and mother was the art teacher until they got me. She then left and just a few days a week she managed to take private tuition from home, which paid well and was ideal. They met at school, in fact father used to say that when she walked into the staffroom for the first time and his eyes fell on her it was love at first sight. Within a year they were married, but sadly could not have a family. To this day, I don't know what the problem was.

I enjoyed my years at school, finished with an A in Geography, a B in Home Economics and a B in English. The only sport I really loved was swimming, at which I won a few medals. Our coach wanted me to become part of the school swimming team, but the early hours of training did not appeal to my parents so I was not encouraged much. Both of them were hoping that I wanted to go to Uni as I had the qualifications, but my heart was in cooking and all I desired was to be a professional chef of the highest degree and make them so proud of me. From a very young age, I had a fascination for cooking and would happily spend hours in the kitchen with my mother as she was a wonderful cook and seemingly my blood mother had been a pâtissière in a French pastry shop, so I suppose it was all in my genes.

2

The Scottish School of Cookery had an excellent reputation and produced some excellent chefs who had become internationally known. It was a two-year course which covered everything in the culinary world.

From the very first day, I loved every minute. It was so rewarding being able to produce such amazing food. I never dreamt how much there was to learn, but I had the drive and sheer determination that I would become a fabulous chef. My parents loved it when I brought home some of my signature dishes which simply astounded them. So over time, they realised that I had chosen the right path and there was no doubt of my talent.

My goal was that, for experience, after I finished, I would get a job in a good restaurant and then, when I felt ready, I would open my own and go from strength to strength, even internationally. I was a very strong person who believed in herself and there was nothing I could not achieve and was quite prepared for long hours and hard work knowing that in the end how I would reap from it all. It was towards my last year that my world came crashing down when the cookery school received a phone call from my mother that my father had an accident and I was to go to the hospital immediately. He had been knocked off his bike by a lorry whilst cycling to the school. The driver claimed that he did not see him and so he was crushed into a barrier by the side of the road.

By the time I got to A&E it was too late. He had died on arrival. My mother met me in a private waiting room where we held onto each other, almost frightened to let go. Our grief was inexplicable. He only had six months to go before he retired and mother and he had made wonderful plans to travel. It was all so utterly cruel and from that day, I knew our lives would never be the same again. I loved him so much I just could not imagine what life would be like without him. He was a friend as well as a father. In fact, I felt as if I had suddenly lost my anchor. As much as I loved my mother, it was he who made me feel so secure that as long as I had him nothing would ever happen to me. And for the first time in my life I had this awful feeling of vulnerability.

Life can be so unjust when someone you love so much leaves you and it has such a devastating effect on those left. I suppose we take people for granted; when you see someone nearly every day of your life it's just normal, but then when you can't, it's unbearable. I have been told that when a loved one dies a light goes out inside you.

I have found that not to be. For me, it has just dimmed a little as when I think of him that light ignites and gives me a moment of comfort.

My poor mother was totally broken hearted and it was months later that I felt something had to be done to help her. Thankfully, Pauline, my closest friend at cookery school, suggested counselling classes as her mother had died and her father had found great solace in them. Pauline and I were more like sisters, we had so much in common and knew that we would be friends for life and would always be there for each other.

3

At the end of my course, I graduated with Honours as top student, a great advantage when looking for a job. I was absolutely delighted when the first job I tried for was with Paul Souter, owner of a Michelin Star restaurant in Edinburgh, who offered me a six month trial starting as a Sous Chef. This was more than I had dreamt of. He had been at our finals and had been very impressed with my work. This was the start to my career, as what I would be able to learn from him would be awesome.

His restaurant was called 'Pauls'. It was just a comfortable size with about forty covers, giving it all a very intimate atmosphere. All the produce was Scottish, specialising in seafood which I loved cooking with. The decor was modern with an open view kitchen. There were wonderful paintings on the walls for sale from local artists. The tables and chairs were in a very dark wood with pure white linen mats and napkins for contrast. Every day a posy of fresh flowers was on each table, along with little t-lights in very unusual holders that looked like a Scottish thistle. Instantly, I felt that I would be very happy here. Like me, Paul was a stickler for detail and I was well aware that this was food at its highest level, with no place for errors at all.

How proud my father would have been. He would have enjoyed coming to 'Pauls' with my mother for dinner, knowing his girl was the chef.

Within no time, my six months were up and, without any hesitation; Paul offered me a permanent job and contract with an excellent salary. I felt quite ecstatic.

Mother was so much better having been at the counselling classes. I didn't feel so guilty leaving her in the evenings whilst I went to work. She was even starting to enjoy her tutoring again which was company for her.

As for me, it really was my job that helped me after father died as there was little time to think of oneself. I had literally thrown myself into the job completely, which was a blessing for me. The only free day I had was a Monday when the restaurant was closed. On these days, I tried to get some form of exercise, either cycling or walking. But it still wasn't enough to lose the few pounds I had acquired since working. I put it down to snacking and late night eating comfort food. What I needed was a good workout and a swim at least once a week. I had a pretty good figure and wanted to keep it that way.

A new fitness club called 'Energy' had opened up quite near the restaurant. The membership wasn't too bad, so for the first few weeks I decided to have a personal trainer to set me right. I was determined to get down to a size twelve again, as being quite tall I really had to look quite slim.

My personal trainer was a great guy from Poland and certainly knew his business. In fact, at times, I called him a sadist! After our workout my swim was sheer heaven and in fact he commented that I had to be one of the strongest and fastest female swimmers he had seen in the club. And to end it all, I would finish with a wonderful massage by one of their therapists. So by the time Tuesday came around I was fighting fit for my week's work.

It seemed that every Monday evening it was mostly the same people, so when we were finished a few of us would meet in the cafe for a get together. It was fun and a change of conversation from food.

Paul kept saying that on a Sunday and Monday I should join a sports club or such like so I may meet someone as he didn't think it was healthy for me not to have any fun. But who on earth would put up with the unsocial hours I had? There had only been a couple of boyfriends at cookery school and the last one became far too possessive and serious. He wanted us to start a small hotel with fine dining on one of the islands up north. I couldn't think of anything worse. Besides that, I felt no love for him. It was purely physical and also he was very volatile and the thoughts of all those knives in a kitchen … no thank you!

Being the philosophical person I am, my thoughts were that one day I would find the right person and start a family. But not until I had achieved my goal of having a most successful restaurant of my own.

All that seemed quite straight forward then. How could I ever have imagined how my life would change, taking me on a horrendously incredulous path in which my life would never be exempt from fear.

It was amazing that I had been attending the club for nearly five months now and thankfully the hard effort was really paying off as my weight was just right and I had never felt fitter.

In the last couple of weeks I had noticed an extremely good looking man, could have been late forties or early fifties. I was never great at judging ages. He was tall and slim with sandy coloured, short, beautifully cut hair. He had quite an aristocratic air about him with very chiselled features. I really had to stop myself from staring at him as it was difficult to keep my eyes off him.

He kept very much to himself, working out mostly on the treadmill and at times with the weights. Unfortunately, he never took to the pool where I thought I may have a chance of meeting him at least. There was something definitely captivating about this man. I started casually enquiring of him but no-one knew anything about him at all, just that he kept himself to himself and came over as quite aloof which for me made him even more interesting.

When it came to a Monday night at the club I found myself longing to see this stranger. In fact, I felt as if I had become a bit of a voyeur. Perhaps in a weird way it felt safer to have this relationship in my mind only as there was every possibility that he was happily married or in some sort of relationship. It would be very unusual for a guy like this to have no attachments, so it was time to stop this nonsense before I made a total idiot of myself. But this was certainly more than a schoolgirl crush that I felt.

The next three weeks passed without him appearing, making me realise how absolutely ridiculous I had been in fantasising about a total stranger. It was quite pathetic.

4

Dr Boyd had been the family dentist. He was a lovely man, so caring with such a fun personality that always made you feel less nervous. I remember it was he who fitted my first set of braces, which I detested! But thankfully it was all worth it as my teeth are all beautifully straight.

It's a bit ironic that our dentist and doctor have retired at the same time. I suppose it's an age thing. They will both be sorely missed and hard to replace, especially Dr Gregor from our medical practice who was more like a family friend and had been wonderful with mother when father died. Father and he used to play golf at least once a month and mother would joke and say that after the golf you would think that father knew more about medicine than Dr Gregor! I remember seeing pictures of father at the golf club when he won the club trophy, mother and I there with him. I always hated having my picture taken when I was young. I think I was a bit of an ugly duckling with bright red hair that I simply hated and legs that looked too skinny. Thank God my hair has now toned down to a lovely titian colour and the legs are pretty good, so I did turn into the swan after all!

Much to my annoyance, the toothache I had been having was definitely not going on its own, so I was forced to make an appointment with Dr Boyd's replacement, a Mr Fletcher. On arriving at the practice, I was greeted warmly by a new receptionist called Megan who was extremely attractive with a lovely personality. I had just started reading a magazine when Megan came to take me through to the surgery. It had all been refurbished since I was last there, looking very smart, painted in light blue and grey.

Our new dentist had his back to me, looking at what I could see were x-rays. He seemed fairly tall and dressed all in blue, almost matching the walls. There was soft classical music playing, all very different from Dr Boyd's day. Mr Fletcher turned and apologised, explaining that he wasn't aware that I had come in. It was then my heart missed not one, but several beats when the man standing in front of me was my fantasy from the gym.

He had the bluest eyes that I had ever seen on a man. They really seemed to penetrate right through me like the x-ray he was watching. I think he may have thought, for a second, I had taken a stroke or such like as I found it difficult to get my tongue round any words correctly. Thankfully, all that was required was a simple filling and I could get out of the surgery and into the fresh air as my legs were feeling very peculiar and my head felt like cotton wool. The only blessing was that he did not recognise me from the gym. Just bloody marvellous. Now I would have to find myself another dentist as there is no way on earth I could put myself through that ever again. How had I longed to meet him but what an introduction this was. It couldn't have been worse if I had tried. God knows what opinion he must have had of me. Just a total nutcase!

It was a Monday and there was no way that I was going to the gym that evening. I just didn't want to face him again, so I would give it a couple of weeks to let me get my head round all of this. I hated feeling that I had made a fool of myself, which was so unlike me. Never had anyone had such an effect on me before.

That evening, mother and I had dinner and shared a bottle of Pinotage, which was her favourite. When I told her my story about the dentist, it was the first time in such a long time that I witnessed her laughing so heartily. At first I felt angry at her finding it so amusing 'til she convinced me to try and see the funny side of it. As she rightly said, I have every right now to start a conversation with him at the gym as, after all, he is my dentist!

Mother knew one of the dental nurses as they went to the same book club. She offered to do a little investigating into Mr Fletcher's marital status, or whatever.

That same evening, mother told me she had met a friend at the counselling classes. His wife had died about the same time as father had. She felt extremely sorry for him as he had no family and was horrendously lonely. They discovered that they had so much in common, i.e. the love of music, theatre and the arts. Although he was certainly a good bit older than she, it did not bother her as she really enjoyed his company. I was so happy for her and delighted to see her more like her old self. She deserved some happiness. Plus the fact it made me feel less guilty about having to leave her alone so much.

The news from the book club was, not married, never had been. Qualified at the Dentistry University of Washington where his father had once taught dental education. Mr Fletcher worked in the States for a short while before coming back to England and had worked in London ever since getting the position here. He had wonderful qualifications and an amazing CV, plus references. The staff at the practice felt they were so lucky to have him.

He rented an apartment just around the corner from the surgery so either walked or cycled to work; he certainly had no need for a car and was extremely popular with the female patients, which did not surprise me one little bit! I was surprised, what with all this information, that mother didn't find out what colour his underpants were!

5

Saturday evenings were always busy in the restaurant, so it was then I did my 'Dish of the Day', which would not be on the menu. Early on in the morning I went to the fish market and bought amazing lobster along with huge scallops. I had decided on Lobster Thermador, one of my signature dishes. Paul was so impressed with it every time he had it. He liked it so much that, with being able to get lobsters all year round and not just seasonally, he wanted to include it in the main menu. Despite being very expensive, customers were quite happy to pay for it.

By the end of the evening, I was utterly shattered as I had been working non-stop and the heat of the kitchen was hellish, even with air conditioning. Just as I was getting ready to call it a day and head home for a very much needed shower and glass of something, our Maitre D' of the restaurant caught me before I had a chance to change out of my whites to say that Table 5 had a request to congratulate the chef. Apparently, it was the most fabulous lobster they had ever had. Much to my dislike, Paul encouraged me to do this as he said it was great PR and customers looked upon us as celebrities and loved meeting us. All I could find was some kitchen towel to wipe my poor dripping face and neck! I had to keep my chef's hat on as by now my hair was just soaking wet from perspiration. I certainly looked a sight!

Table Five was a cosy little table for two tucked away in an alcove. Most romantic. As I approached the table, the gentleman stood up to greet me. As his guest had her back to me, I couldn't make out who she was, but my God there was no mistaking who he was.

Tony Fletcher looked so bloody handsome in a navy blazer and open neck pink shirt. In that moment all I prayed for was the ground to open up and swallow me. This had to be my 'Bridget Jones' moment. And, of course, to finish it off, his gorgeous dinner date was dear Megan the receptionist, looking stunning. She must have thought I resembled the lobster as my face by this time was puce.

He congratulated me and offered me a glass of champagne which, of course, I declined. Being in no mood for pathetic chit chat, I politely wished them a lovely evening and got the hell out of there. I still didn't know if he recognised me at all from his surgery or the gym. Why would he anyway? I was of no interest to him at all.

6

My decision was to look for another gym as, frankly, I did not want to see Tony Fletcher again. My mind was made up. No good was going to come out of this stupid fixation I had for him. It was time to move on.

A couple of weeks passed when, one busy lunch time, a magnificent bouquet of flowers was delivered to me from 'Fleur' the florist. Of course, this caused great excitement for everyone! I couldn't think of a single living person who would send me flowers like this! The last time I ever got flowers was on Valentine's Day, back when I was at college, from my boyfriend whom I haven't seen for years anyway. But for an unknown reason, I could feel butterflies in my stomach as I opened up the card. "Please come to dinner on Monday 19th, 7.30pm at Gino's. Regards, Tony". For a moment I could not believe my eyes. I just didn't know what to think! One thing was for sure – it wasn't that he fancied me! Especially after our last encounter! I had no possible idea what his motive could be. Perhaps he felt sorry for me in some way. My God! That I could not tolerate under any circumstances!

By now Wendy, one of our waitresses, was almost beside herself with excitement. Apparently, she had waited on him several times in the restaurant, but he had never had the same girl with him twice. Quite the ladies' man, I thought. My first reaction was a definite no. But after a great deal of persuasion from Paul and co, I decided to go. They said I would be a fool not to go as I had nothing to lose by it. Anyway, this would probably put him right out of my system once and for all. But somehow, deep down in my gut, I had the feeling that this was a big mistake and may end in tears.

It was time that I spent some money on myself as I really was in need of a total makeover. In the last few months, I had neglected my appearance, or so I was often told by my mother.

So, Mr Fletcher, if this is a token of goodwill dinner for some poor soul then you are in for one goddamn surprise! I will leave you speechless. It's time the tables were turned.

The first task was off to a very good boutique where I bought a snazzy little black dress. It was quite short with long sleeves and looked rather demure until you turn round and see it is backless. Just fantastic. I felt a million dollars in it. There was a pair of high heel shoes in black suede which I just could not resist to compliment my dress. I never imagined I could spend so much money, but what the hell, I was earning a damn good salary and it was time to spend on myself.

I purchased some fabulous make up from the beauty consultant after I had my makeover done. Then off to my hairdresser for the finishing off the new me. Michael was a marvellous stylist. He cut my hair to a swinging bob and put fantastic auburn highlights through my hair.

Monday 19th was here and as I stood looking at myself in the mirror, even I was amazed at how incredibly different I looked which, to sum up, was utterly fantastic. When I came downstairs to call a taxi, mother took one look at me and her eyes filled with tears. She thought I looked truly beautiful and talked about how proud father would have been to see me as he always said one day I would turn an eye or two.

We had a glass of wine together whilst waiting for my cab to steady my nerves and it was then I realised that I had been a bit heavy on the Chanel, but what the hell!

The taxi was booked for 7.30pm, so I would arrive after him as the last thing I wanted was to be there first, as I had imagined my entrance so many times.

Gino and his wife, the owners of the restaurant, were a lovely Italian couple whom I had met before. The food was excellent, with authentic Italian cuisine. And to add to it, they always had such romantic Italian music playing softly in the background. But the only times I had visited had been with my mother and some friends, so that was a waste.

As I approached the restaurant, I really took cold feet big time and was just about to ask the driver to take me home when suddenly we were there. There was no turning back now as Gino was already out opening the door for me. If only I had turned back. How different my life may have been.

Gino greeted me warmly with, "Bella! Bella!" I think even Gino got quite a surprise at the transformation. He put his arm through mine in a fatherly way and led me to the table where Tony Fletcher was waiting. It was as if I had written the script. His reaction was more than I had imagined. He leapt up and obviously got such a shock that he knocked over a wine glass. I could not have orchestrated this any better! After he quickly composed himself, he kissed me on both cheeks before asking me to take a seat. Simply taking everything about me in, he complimented me on how I looked. Strangely, I did not need his compliments, as I knew how stunning I was, especially when one or two heads turned as I walked in with Gino, giving me the confidence I wanted.

Before he said a word, a bottle of Bollinger Champagne appeared. It did cross my mind that it would have been correct to ask me what I would like as an aperitif, even if this was more than acceptable.

We both ordered Salmone Formaggi to start, followed by Scaloppina Fantasia accompanied by a very expensive Amarone Della Valpolicella Classico.

During the evening, we were amazed just how much in common we had, from food to music and even politics. I felt so relaxed in his company. It was as if we had known each other for years. He had a wonderful sense of humour, something I always thought was so important in a man. I was beginning to find Tony Fletcher rather intoxicating. In fact, the chemistry between us was incredible. He certainly had some charisma.

After dinner, Tony organised a taxi to take both of us home. Firstly me and then himself. While we sat in the taxi close together he held my hand, which seemed to send a shockwave through me. Then, without a word, he turned my face to his and kissed me. It was like nothing I had experienced before. And with a quiet word to the driver, we just headed for his flat.

7

As the months passed, I became more and more in love with Tony. In fact, I had acquired quite an insatiable appetite for him. We were with no doubt an item. Tony had never been so much in love before, I was what he always wanted. I could not believe how deliriously happy I was, almost terrified that my bubble would burst. Tony was such fun and exciting to be with, although at times a little over dramatic. But this was something I was able to cope with. In fact, I often thought he had missed his vocation and should have gone on the stage.

There was no doubt at all in my mind that I had found my soulmate and before long, he would ask me to marry him. My future was planned out for me in that perhaps Tony may want to move and have his own dental practice and I could open my own restaurant wherever he wanted to settle. Then, in time, we would start a family.

Tony had no sisters or brothers, but both parents were still alive, living in Crystal River, Florida. He didn't see much of them, perhaps once a year. I got the feeling he was much closer to his mother as his father was quite domineering. He never forgave him for not wanting to practice in America. And not fully understanding Tony, his father had always been extremely hard on him when he was just a young boy. He could never match up to his father's expectations. Even to this day, he would never admit to being proud of Tony, despite what Tony had accomplished in dentistry.

For about a week, I had become aware of a slight change in Tony's mood. He was much quieter, as if something was on his mind. But when I asked if there was a problem we could share, worrying it could be some sort of health issue, he was adamant that was not the case. I got the vibes to drop it and let it sort itself out.

A few days later he declared he was going to London for an appointment and would explain everything when he came home. I certainly got the feeling not to ask any questions, which actually hurt me as I thought we were so close. I thought we had no secrets from each other.

I knew that I would have a knot in my stomach until he returned and put me out of my misery. I just could not understand the secrecy of it all. So many explanations crossed my mind, all of which worried me even more.

He flew down to London early one Thursday morning. He told me he would be returning early evening. That day in the restaurant, I found it so difficult to concentrate on my cooking and simply longed to finish my shift so I could head for his flat. All the time, I wasn't able to get rid of a squeamish feeling that somehow I was not going to like what this was about.

Tony opened his door with the biggest smile on his face, a smile I hadn't seen for a while. Instantly, I knew I had my old Tony back. So whatever this was about, it had gone to his liking. Sitting on the glass coffee table was a bucket with a bottle of champagne.

Instantly, like a lightning bolt had struck me, I realised

this was what I dreamed of. Tony was going to propose to me and this is what it had all been about. Of course! He must have had to think about it so much and the London visit was to buy the ring from a friend who I knew he once mentioned worked in Hatton Gardens. It made so much sense! It was almost impossible to restrain myself from shouting 'Yes, Yes, Yes' before he got the chance to ask me.

But, oh my God, how wrong could I have been. The feeling I had was as if I had just crashed back down to earth again. It was impossible not to show the huge disappointment in my face, but Tony was on such a high I doubt if he even noticed.

A couple of weeks before, he had seen a job application for a dental posting with the American Embassy in Tangier, Morocco. The embassy in London had been extremely impressed with his CV and were keen to meet him. He flew down for an interview after which they offered him the post there and then as he was the perfect dentist for the job. He really had impressed them with his expertise in orthodontics.

The bubbly was opened, but it was strange having been so close to someone and yet they fail to sense the lack of enthusiasm or sheer shock in the eyes of their loved one. All I could think was where the hell did I come in to this equation? If at all. Finding myself in the situation, I really didn't want to ask about us as it was surely up to Tony to clarify what was going to happen with our relationship. But if he asked me to go with him then that's what I would do. I personally did not care where he went. I just wanted us to be together forever.

Within no time, Tony made things very clear. He would be taking up the post almost immediately and I was to go out for a spell and see what I thought of it all. End of story. No talk of marriage, or at least commitment. My pride held me back from asking what his intentions were. I felt so utterly gutted. I had been such a fool that I had read so much more into our relationship.

My only consolation was that perhaps he would not make a commitment until he was established for once. And time apart would make him realise he couldn't live without me. As long as it wasn't out of sight, out of mind!

It was strange that the only person who did not rate Tony was Paul. He said he was far too egotistical for his own good and I deserved better. Of course, I used to laugh this off.

8

As the months passed, it became very evident that Tony just loved his job and the way of life in Tangier. He had to adjust to different working hours, fitting in early morning appointments and not finishing until nearly 7.30pm at least. So by the time he got home he was pretty tired. There was only one dentist working with him. Stephen was a young America, but did not have the same experience or qualifications as Tony had which put pressure on Tony as he was taking on all the intricate work. There was a female hygienist who was French which worried me a little. Such a cosy cosmopolitan scene. I felt ashamed that I didn't trust Tony, but I knew how women may come on to him and could only hope he would resist temptation. He certainly gave me no cause for jealousy when we were together.

Tony tried emailing as much as he could and would send me pictures of the villa he was staying in, along with shots of the embassy and parts of Tangier.

Eight months passed and still no word from Tony about me going out to Tangier. I discussed with Paul when the best time for me to go would be and we both agreed sooner than later before the festive season started. So, literally within a couple of weeks I could be off to see him.

Much to my disappointment, Tony suggested that I waited and perhaps went out for Christmas, but he knew the scene with the restaurant and that it would be impossible so heavens knows what he was thinking of.

My mind was made up and nothing was going to stop me. I had come to a crossroads in my life and one way or other I had to know what the future held for me. If I was to make my life in Tangier, so be it. I could certainly start a little restaurant there.

Missing Tony was an understatement. I felt such an enormous void in my life. So knowing that in a couple of weeks we would be reunited was an awesome feeling. It was the only thing to keep my intact.

9

Morocco

My flight was booked with an open ticket. Flying Edinburgh to London then on to Tangier. There was quite a mix of passengers, as well as some tourists and locals. All very cosmopolitan.

As the thud of the wheels hit the runway so also did my stomach. I was so full of excitement yet had this awful feeling of trepidation as well which was just so ridiculous. I knew once I saw Tony I could put all this nonsense behind me. All I needed was the reassurance of his love for me.

The plane doors opened and the warm night air wafted in with a soft breeze carrying the scent of jasmine.

As I entered the baggage area I felt that it was another world. With all the Arabian gentlemen in their flowing white robes I had certainly come to where East meets the West

I could see my case coming, but with such a crowd grabbing at bags I had to wait for it to appear second time round. Just as I tried to make a lunge for it, the most gracious and handsome young Arabian man got it for me, placed it in my trolley and asked if I was meeting anyone as his driver would be more than happy to take me wherever I was going. After declining his kind offer he kissed my hand and wished me a safe and pleasant stay in his country. The mind boggled as to where that could have led to.

The arrivals hall was just a sea of faces from every part of the world. My eyes were frantically trying to spot Tony when suddenly I heard my name being shouted above the crowd. At last I was able to see Tony. As I pushed my way through and came face to face with him it was then I was so taken aback at how much his appearance had changed. For a start, he looked older and had lost quite a bit of weight. His hair was so much longer and fairer, obviously bleached by the sun, and I could see silver streaks through it. It looked incredible against his tan. He was wearing a blue checked shirt and white chinos with the most expensive looking blue suede loafers. He really was quite something. One would have thought he had lived in Tangier all his life.

My welcome wasn't exactly the huge embrace I envisaged whilst sitting on the plane. Instead, I got a bear hug and a kiss on the cheek, as if I was some old long lost friend.

As we came out of the airport a huge black Mercedes pulled up and two men jumped out. One held the door open for an Arabian gentleman, while the other got in beside the driver. Much to my surprise, I caught a glimpse and saw it was the charming young man that had offered me a lift. I noticed a flag on the front of the car with some sort of crest on it.

When I asked Tony if he knew who it could be, he thought it was the young Prince Karim who had been educated at Oxford and had business connections in London where he travels to frequently. Apparently, he is often in the paper with his radical ideas for Morocco, such as only believing in one wife and such life. Well, I thought that may have been a very interesting little journey if I had taken up his offer.

Crossing the road to where cars were parked, Tony took out a key and at the bleep, two huge red lights flashed. It certainly was quite a shock that this was his car. It was a beautiful white convertible BMW that must have cost the earth. For someone who was never into cars before, this was quite an eye opener. I just got the picture of Tony driving around Tangier and with his looks it sure would get some attention! It was so obvious this car was his pride and joy.

The drive from the airport was, I felt, full of polite conversation regarding his job, the people in the embassy and total love for Tangier. In fact, at last he felt he had found his Shangri-La. As we drove through Tangier, I had to admit, even at night with all the lights along the Boulevard, there was something magical about it. Not far from the town, we turned into a pretty tree-lined avenue and stopped outside a charming terracotta-coloured villa. There were elaborate iron gates with a stone plaque that had "Villa Bedouzza" on it. A long path led to an extremely heavy looking wooden door with two huge tubs on either side full of lovely colourful plants. Above the door were two black iron lanterns which were lit.

The villa was owned by the American Embassy and Tony was paying an extraordinarily cheap rent for such a lovely habitat, no wonder he wasn't anxious to look for something else. This was his for as long as he wanted.

He opened the door and facing me was a spacious round hall with mosaic tiles on the floor with a stone staircase up to the bedrooms. The lounge area had two large settees in cream-coloured linen with a long, wooden, carved coffee table. There were French windows that I presumed led out to a garden. At first glance it was very clinical and I thought it really could have done with a woman's touch. As for the kitchen, it looked as if it was hardly ever used, or Tony had a wizard cleaner as the whole villa was spotless.

As it was so late, Tony suggested a nightcap and bed as he had had a very busy day and felt shattered. He was also up early in the morning. When we got into bed, Tony kissed my cheek and turned on his side and fell sound asleep, just lying beside him like that after all this time was not at all natural. No matter how tired he was, it had never stopped him making love before. It was that first night that things felt different, but I was not ready to admit to myself something was not right.

10

I awoke early with the sound of a cockerel crowing and the sun streaming through the window. Tony was already up and I could smell the gorgeous aroma of fresh coffee wafting up the stairs.

There was orange juice, croissants and coffee already set up on the patio for me and Tony was dressed and ready to leave for the embassy. He wished for me to use his precious car during the day as he had purchased a bike that he took to the embassy as it was his only way of exercise.

The garden was so pretty and colourful, with a large gazebo covered in Bougainvillea at the far end of the garden. It was all so beautifully manicured.

Just as Tony was about to leave, a young Arabian boy arrived from the side of the villa carrying tools. Tony went up to him and spoke to him in Arabic which completely amazed me. I wondered how on earth he had the time to learn the language. He brought the boy over to me and introduced us. The boy's name was Askim. He was one of the gardeners at the embassy and also looked after the embassy properties.

Askim was simply delightful. So polite and actually spoke quite good English. He certainly was no more than seventeen with almost too pretty a face. He asked me if there was anything I wished him to do around the villa and he said he would be more than happy to help.

My decision was not to take the car as it was such a wonderful day and I needed a walk, so I headed up into Tangier as it wasn't far from the villa. It only took me twenty minutes to walk up to the main boulevard we drove through on the evening I arrived. It looked so different in daylight. So much bigger than I had thought. There were enormous palm trees swaying gently in the balmy breeze. The cafes and boutiques were bustling and the place was so alive with activity. After a while, I stopped at a cafe for a coffee and watched the world go by.

Every nationality in the world must have passed me by. It was so interesting. Somehow I didn't feel like a tourist, it was strange. It seemed as if I had been there for years. I was so at ease and felt like I could certainly live there once Tony got over his midlife crisis, if that's what it was.

I knew he could be moody which I accepted, but this was different. After how close we had been, I really did not know this person that I had fallen in love with. There was some sort of barrier between us and I was most determined to break it down.

Venturing along to the harbour, I saw some amazing little yachts and some fantastic cruisers. I hate to think what they would have cost. The sound was lovely, with the halyards tinkling in the breeze.

On my way back, I was interested in seeing the market, especially the fresh catch of the day coming in. It reminded me of home and going for my lobsters. The jumbo prawns looked wonderful and I couldn't resist buying a few for our dinner. Having looked in his fridge before I left, I saw nothing that would make a decent meal. He would be in for a treat tonight, I thought.

When I arrived back at the villa, I was struck by the heavenly scent of flowers that had been put in a vase in the lounge. I also saw a big basket of fresh fruit in the kitchen, along with a little pot of freshly cut herbs. Instantly, the place looked like a home being lived in. I was so amazed as the only person who could have done this kind gesture was Askim. It really touched me to think how thoughtful and kind this young man was.

I enjoyed preparing a beautiful dinner of artichokes with melted butter followed by prawn provencal with saffron rice. The table was set with a candle that I found. It all looked very romantic and I had made an effort with my appearance. I looked pretty good in my new silver-grey, linen, palazzo trousers with a white silk tunic. I had my fingers crossed it would do the trick

Whenever he walked in the door I could see how genuinely tired he looked. But after a shower and a couple of dry martinis, something that was always a great favourite of his, he seemed to revive. However, this was certainly not the right time for deep discussions. I knew I would have to pick my moment which, for me, was utterly crazy, having had the sort of relationship we had that I was able to talk over anything. But now I felt as if I was walking on broken glass.

After dinner I went into the kitchen to make coffee and when I returned Tony was just stretched out on the settee sound asleep, so I just threw a rug over him and that's where he remained until morning.

As the days passed it started to occur to me that there

may well be a health reason for his tiredness and strange behaviour. However, it came as a surprise when I asked him if he would have a check-up and perhaps a blood test and he agreed. Apparently, there was a Dr Simon Jeffrey at the embassy who he regarded highly.

It crossed my mind that if we had a party then I could meet most of his friends from the embassy and I thought a little entertaining would be good for us on a social level. Thankfully, Tony agreed knowing that I would take it in hand and do everything. All he was going to do was ask about a dozen or so people that he wanted.

11

The one place I had not ventured to was the medina, the old town, which was a walled city. Tony had warned me to watch myself as it was a haven for pick pockets, especially a female on her own without a guide. But by now I really felt quite streetwise. On my list of things to buy from the party was a clay tagine cooking pot and I was sure I would get an excellent one at the market. On entering the souk, which was a labyrinth of alleys, I was struck by how intoxicating it felt with the amazing aromas of incense from the musk, orange flower and so on. Just a total expression of senses.

I wandered past the stalls of leather with wonderfully coloured pouffes and wonderful cushions in all colours, shapes and sizes. All obviously made locally. This certainly was a cultural experience not to be missed, the vibrancy of the souk was incredible. The music straight from *Arabian Nights*. I just loved every ounce of it all.

Luckily I came across the ceramics and purchased my tagine, but I could not resist buying some spices, saffron and dried fruits. They were so much cheaper than back home. On my way out, there was a little stand selling handmade jewellery where I bought my mother and I a silver bracelet with the hand of Fatima hanging on it which supposedly gives you protection. Little did I know how I would need it!

At the entrance to the souk there was a group of Rif women who came down from the mountains dressed in spectacular, colourful, traditional costumes selling their handcrafted wears. I bought a couple of beautiful baskets I thought would be perfect for the party to put my homemade bread in.

I had a strange feeling when leaving the souk that I may never be back. It had been such a wonderful experience that I could almost lose myself and my problems for a short time it certainly was totally captivating.

The day before the party, Tony told me that he had had a check up and the blood tests were all fine. It was put down to being overworked, so I suggested we took the car for a few days and drive down the coast to Casablanca to give him a rest, but that did not appeal to him

Mostly everyone that Tony had invited had accepted and I was looking forward to meeting all of the guests, including the American dentist and Dr Jeffrey and his daughter who was a marine biologist in Tangier.

On the day of the party, I worked solidly, non-stop, cooking my lamb tagine and preparing amazing salads and desserts. It was while I was working in the kitchen pulling out knives that I came across a little card with a tiny monkey on it and the name 'Marco Polio Bar'. Tony had never mentioned it before, to take me for a drink or such like, so I decided not to mention it and perhaps pay it a little visit on my own sometime. It definitely had been put out of sight, I thought, hidden under all the cutlery.

I had bought some Riad Jamil wines which I was sure would go down well, but to start, I made up a rather potent punch with masses of fresh mint and fruit to get things going.

Askim arrived and as usual was wonderful. He set up the bar and tables for me, leaving me more time to give the finishing touches to my canapes.

When I went upstairs to the bedroom to change, on the bed was a large box with 'Jolie Madam' on it which I knew was a very exclusive boutique in Tangier. I had been in once, but found it was all designer labels and it was way out of my pocket.

I opened the box and amongst beautiful red tissue paper scented by scattered rose petals there was a little card that simply read "Thank you". Under the tissues I lifted out the most beautiful pure silk kaftan with delicate beading round the low neck. The colours of the kaftan were in burnt orange and antique gold which were just my colours. It was utterly gorgeous. I couldn't have picked anything better for myself. He really had exquisite taste for a man and at a price.

Having never worn anything like this I was amazed how cool the silk felt on the skin. Just total luxury. It was fantastic on me and I felt so wonderful with it on. My gold cascade earrings were just the right accompaniment to finish off the Moroccan look.

When I came down the stairs, Askim was busy polishing glasses and I could tell by the expression on his face that he was more than impressed.

Tony was waiting on the patio with two glasses of champs for us to have before our guests arrived. It was the first time that I saw his face light up. He was so delighted at how I looked in his gift and that I loved it. For a brief moment, we actually had eye contact and it was then he quietly said "sorry" but before I could answer, our first guests had arrived and that very precious moment was broken. All through the party I just kept hearing the word "sorry" in my head and thinking what the hell does it all mean? He certainly had a great deal to feel sorry about.

The people from the embassy were a lovely bunch. They were really good fun and so easy to make friends with, especially Dr Jeffrey who was quite the character. On taking the opportunity, I thanked him for looking after Tony and how relieved I was that the blood test and everything was fine. But the expression on his face said it all. It was so obvious he hadn't a bloody clue about what I was talking about. I really felt that I had embarrassed him as he changed the subject instantly. This wasn't just patient confidentiality. It was clear Tony had never been to see him at all.

My head was thumping as I knew Tony had told me a barefaced lie and I felt such a fool. If only I hadn't opened my mouth: I would be none the wiser instead of feeling so very hurt and angry.

12

I started to feel that this definitely was not the man whom I had fallen in love with and the distance between us was certainly not improving.

It was Tony's late night at the surgery and I felt bored out of mind with far too much time on my hands, so I decided it was time to see the Marco Polio Bar for myself.

I ordered a taxi as there was no way I would take the car. The driver was an older man with long grey hair tied in a ponytail and had little tortoiseshell spectacles. He certainly looked a real character. He spoke perfect English and came over as being very polite. When I told him where I wanted to go, he seemed rather surprised and asked if I had been before and if I was meeting a friend there.

We drove through parts of Tangier that I had never seen before. Definitely well out of the tourist zone. At the end of an alleyway we stopped outside a neon light sign flashing 'Marco Polio Bar' with an arrow pointing to a basement down some very worn stone steps. Upon leaving the taxi, the old boy gave me his card and asked me to call him when I wanted to go back as it would not be advisable to wander round looking for a taxi in this area.

I carefully descended the narrow steps to a dark green painted door that had seen better days. Once I opened it, I had to adjust my eyes to the smoke screen and my ears to the incredible noise of music. How anyone could hear themselves talk I'll never know: it seemed that shouting was the only way.

The bar was full of the strangest looking people I had ever seen. At a quick glance, I would think they were all Moroccan with a few exceptions. I just couldn't imagine what Tony would have in common with any of them, especially one or two who looked utterly undesirable characters.

The man behind the bar was heavy set with a shaved head and huge gold hoop earrings. He had dark, swarthy skin and a little black beard. Straight out of *Pirates of the Carribean*, especially with the tiny monkey dressed in a scarlet waistcoat and the little fez on its head. The monkey sat mostly on his shoulder then would quickly dive down on the bar and take a handful of nuts.

Under different circumstances I would have found these antics hysterical, but all I wanted was a stiff drink and to get out, as I could see some strange looks coming from one or two people. I was definitely a new face and must have looked utterly uncomfortable. As I quickly drank a vodka on ice surrounded by a mist of cigarette smoke, I suddenly saw through an enormous gilt-edged mirror behind the back of the bar, the face of Tony. He was sitting with a few people, none of whom I recognised from the party. This was one scene that there was no way I would intrude upon. As I hastily got up to leave, a strange voice was shouting repeatedly "F-off" and when I turned round there was an enormous cage with a parrot eyeballing me. I did wonder if it said that to everyone that left, or whether it took a personal dislike to me! Anyhow, I did exactly as it requested.

As I travelled back to the house, I wondered if this was another lie. Was the once per week late night that Tony told me he worked at the embassy actually a visit to the Marco Polio Bar? My mind was made up that I needed a couple of days away to try and clear my head, so I decided I would take the car and drive to Casablanca.

I kept thinking how Tony preferred to spend time with those strange people instead of me. It was becoming blatantly obvious now that he no longer had the desire to be with me, which was breaking my heart. God only knows where I went wrong. I could not have given him anymore love if I had tried.

My plan was to leave early the next morning before it got too hot. Tony seemed more than delighted that I was doing this, certainly no suggestion of joining me.

I was up early ready to set off when the post arrived. I usually just threw this on the kitchen table, but one letter fell to the ground and upon picking it up I noticed 'Personal and Confidential' written on it in red print. It looked rather foreboding and if it hadn't been for the fact that Tony was lying to me, I never, in a million years, would have been tempted to open it.

Once opened, I could not believe what I was reading:

Dear Mr Fletcher,
Your appointment has been changed to Monday 16th October at 10am. We hope this will not inconvenience you.
Sincerely,
The Clinic of Sexually Transmitted Diseases

I read it several times hoping there was a mistake, but it was not so. My hands were trembling trying to place it back in the envelope to try and re-seal it. My mind was spinning, wondering with whom and where he had contracted a disease from. Was it some female in the embassy he was having a relationship with? It all started to make sense now, but at least, thank God, he had the decency not to make love to me. But that didn't help the tremendous hurt and betrayal I was feeling.

13

So now I understood what the word sorry was all about. I just wondered for a moment did he have a feeling of remorse.

Thankfully, I was able to get away for a couple of days so I could think this one out as confronting him I would certainly let myself down, with him knowing I must have opened the letter. But the way I was feeling, I really didn't care what he would think of me as none of this was my doing.

The drive down the coast in the open top BMW with the wind in my hair and the warm breeze caressing my face was just what I needed. My first stop was Rabat where I was staying in a boutique hotel called Hotel Kenzi Basma. I arrived in time to go sightseeing, then I was in need of a body massage and an early night.

The next morning I went on to Casablanca where I planned on spoiling myself as I thought I definitely deserved it. The Riad Souss in Casablanca was quite famous, a beautiful old Moroccan style hotel where the rich and famous would stay and although I was neither, I loved every minute of it.

In the morning, after I had seen as much of Casablanca as I wanted, I decided to go back to Tangier rather than staying another night, even if Tony was not expecting me. What the hell did it matter anyway? My mind was made up and, one way or another, Tony had plenty of explaining to do. There was no way I was going on with anymore pretence at any cost.

It was late afternoon when I arrived back and I was rather surprised when I saw Tony's bike inside the gate. He certainly had never come home this early any time I had been there. My only thought was that he might have been unwell.

On entering the villa there was no sign of him anywhere. It wasn't until I was in the kitchen and the patio doors were open that I could hear voices coming from the garden. Although the light was fading fast, I could see two figures at the top of the garden under the pergola. It was definitely Tony's voice amidst some laughter. I quietly walked up the path to where I could see, to my utter horror, Tony completely naked in an embrace with someone. I stood rigid to the spot, not believing my eyes as I was just able to see that the other naked person was Askim.

I turned and ran into the villa, just making the toilet before I was sick. My body was trembling and all I was able to think about was getting out of the villa as there was no way on earth I ever wanted to see Tony Fletcher again.

I bolted upstairs and grabbed my belongings, hoping beyond hope that they wouldn't come back in before I was gone. I had never moved so fast in my life. I had a quick check that my passport was in my bag and then ran down the stairs. Without even thinking, I snatched the car keys from the kitchen table and I was out.

Once I was out of the avenue I stopped to gather my senses and tried to calm down enough to make a plan. All

I knew was that I wanted out of Tangier that night. It was too late to head for the airport and the possibility of getting a flight was not good.

The fastest way out at this time would be a ferry over to Gibraltar from Port of Tarifa. I still had time to catch one as I knew they sailed every hour. I drove to the port to see the *Mons Caple* ferry still there. People were starting to board her, so there was no time to spare.

I parked the car and ran for my ticket. At the entrance to boarding the ferry there were traders selling all sorts of wares. But it was a young man who was a snake charmer that caught my eye. He looked so emaciated: there were only a few dirhams in a small copper plate beside the basket where the cobra was rising up to the sound of the pungi that he was playing.

It suddenly came to me that I could not change the world, but perhaps one person's world and a few dirhams dropped in to a plate would not. I stopped in front of him and asked him his name to which he replied, "Asal, Madame."

I then said, "Well, Asal, do you drive?"

With a quizzical expression, he replied, "Yes, Madame."

As I put the keys of the BMW on to his plate I pointed to the car that was parked nearby. He stared at me in total disbelief and quietly said, "Thank you, and may Allah bless you."

When I got on board the ferry, I went up to the top deck and was just in time to see the dust from the tyres of the BMW disappear from the harbour. My snake charmer was gone.

As the ferry pulled out of the port it was dark and all I

could see were lights flickering in Tangier. It was time to say goodbye to Morocco forever.

14

While on the ferry to Gibraltar, I was able to take time and try and get my head around the whole scenario. It all felt like a nightmare. It is such a true saying how love can turn to hate and that's exactly how I was feeling. It would have been kinder if Tony had broken our relationship while he was away, even if I was heartbroken it would have been better than what I endured in Tangier.

After one and a half hours I arrived in Gibraltar and went straight to the Rock Hotel. I knew the manager there as he had been the assistant manager at the Highlands Hotel in Scotland and I hoped he would find me accommodation, even if it wasn't at The Rock.

Thankfully, Peter was still on duty and I was able to have a large room with a balcony. Standing on the balcony looking out, I could see the lights of Tangier in the far distance. It was difficult to comprehend what had happened there in such a short space of time.

I was surprised with myself as I thought I would be crying my eyes out, almost inconsolable. But somehow I felt I would not waste my tears on Tony Fletcher and instead I would move on with my life, even if this had been a bitter pill to swallow. But one thing was for sure, I would never allow myself to be hurt again. This had most certainly left its mark.

In the morning, I was lucky enough to reserve a flight to

London with British Airways at 2.30pm. Before I left for London I contacted my girlfriend, Pauline Webster, who was married to Gordon, a very successful city banker. When Pauline had left the cookery school she had gone down to London and eventually opened up her own extremely lucrative catering business called 'Exclusive Entertaining'. She mainly catered for corporate receptions with a theme, as well as board meetings and lunches.

It wasn't surprising that it was a huge success as in college she, like me, was a perfectionist. Only the best would do and she had an amazing eye for detail.

Pauline was so delighted to hear from me and, just like a true friend, had plenty of TLC to give. She and Gordon insisted that I stay with them for a day or two until I was ready to go home.

Their townhouse was in Kensington, almost behind Harrods. The basement had been converted for her business and the whole operation was so wonderfully professional and impressive with three full time staff plus herself. Yet she was still looking for one more member to complete the team.

The next couple of days were just what was required as Pauline had me straight in there helping her. We had always worked well together and still did. I really loved every minute of it as it was such a different challenge to what I was used to.

Pauline made me promise that I would consider joining her company if things did not work out at home, even if it was a stopgap before I decided exactly what I wanted to do.

Gordon assured me that he would be able to secure funding for me if I did want to start my own small restaurant, even if it wasn't in London. And as Pauline pointed out, with her company I would be meeting some influential and affluent people, something that could be advantageous for me.

15

Once I returned home and had been back at the restaurant for a couple of weeks, I was well aware that my life had changed and that it was no longer for me. There were too many memories that I was not able to put behind me in the environment of 'Paul's' and the gym. I felt so desperately unsettled and my mood swings were not fair on my mother and colleagues at the restaurant.

The time was right to move on. Mother was seeing more and more of George, in fact I knew it would just be a matter of time before they got married. She was happy for me to spread my wings and confessed that she had never really liked Tony. She felt there were two sides to him and didn't trust him. How right she was.

Paul was actually the one who was most upset as he had hoped to retire and hand the restaurant over to me at some point in the near future.

Pauline was so delighted that I was taking up her offer. She insisted that I stayed in their Granny flat at the top of the house which was totally self-contained and would give me my independence and privacy. The rent was so ridiculously cheap compared to the wonderful salary I would be getting. It was most certainly an offer I could not refuse; at least until I knew exactly what path I would take.

Living in London was marvellous. I loved every bit of the buzz and excitement it held. I really felt alive again and had finally moved on with life.

In the first two months we had been so busy with functions and business parties, I also had quite a few invitations to dinner from some men that I met through our work. But that was the last thing I needed, even if Pauline tried to convince me to attend a harmless dinner date with one or two of them. But I had most definitely changed. It was as if there was an invisible barrier around me and I knew it may be a long time before someone could gain my trust again. Until then, I would be the one to call the shots.

There was great excitement in 'Exclusive Entertaining' as we were catering for 'Walker and Jones', a very upmarket travel agents specialising in custom-made holidays to Africa (mostly Kenya, Tanzania and Botswana). The party was to be held in their Mayfair premises and we would be catering for about one hundred people.

The evening was called 'The African Experience' which was to set the theme.

This was a wonderful challenge for us and it had to be absolutely perfect as the guest list was more than impressive, to say the least. Walker and Jones gave us carte blanche to do what we wanted to do in order to transform their travel agents. They were spending serious money on the party.

Pauline and I had long discussions about how we were going to create 'The African Experience' and what type of canapes we would make that would really take them by storm. I made an appointment with the PR of the Botswana Embassy who was more than happy to co-operate with us.

Everyone was totally amazed at what I was given, even

though I had to use my charm for certain objects. I was introduced to the ambassador who insisted that we have coffee together. He was the most charming gentleman from Gaborone and had lived in London for five years with his family. He certainly tried to encourage me to go to Botswana some time for a holiday, something that was definitely most appealing.

His secretary was on the invitation list to promote their country, along with a few dignitaries. Pauline had contacted the top magazines for their social pages as it certainly was to be a very glamorous occasion. Plenty of bling and all that!

On the morning of the party, Pauline and I took our African artefacts to Walker and Jones. She had bought beautiful bunches of Protea and other dried African flowers to make exotic arrangements with.

We placed the large ebony hippos and elephants strategically amongst the zebra rugs and covered the tables with colourful African cloths. When we were finished, the whole effect was utterly spectacular. We had more than achieved our 'African Experience'.

The staff that we had hired for a catering agency to hand round the canapes were dressed in khaki trousers and skirts with white shirts, which looked so much in keeping with the theme.

Walker and Jones were more than delighted. They said what we had created had been beyond their expectations, even down to the amazing African music in the background which added to the incredible ambiance.

As the champagne and canapes were being taken round,

a film was being shown of elephant back safaris, photographic and horse riding ones, as well as everything else that was on offer for the perfect adventure holiday.

If this did not tempt anyone, nothing would. I, for one, was totally sold on it all and this was more than definite for me when I could afford it at some time in my life. It certainly held a strong allure for me.

Pauline introduced me to a couple called Pat and David Masters who had a company in Botswana named Elite Safaris. They were very well respected and successful, with three camps. It was clear they would do amazing business at an evening like the one we were hosting. They had been more than impressed with my work and were interested to hear of my time at 'Paul's'. As was I equally impressed upon hearing about their operation in Botswana, which was so fascinating. It sounded like an amazing life and how privileged they were to live in such surroundings.

The evening had been a huge success for everyone, with great job satisfaction for me.

One of the guests that I recognised from TV and the media was Lisa Scott. She was quite a culinary celebrity as she had a famous 'Hostess Cookery School' in London where most of the debutantes would go to learn how to cook and entertain before marrying into society.

I was rather surprised when she actually approached me and asked if at any time I may be interested in a teaching position as she had admired the work that I had done.

She handed me her card and asked me to contact her, but even as much as I liked her, there was no way I wanted that scene. But it was still flattering.

The day after the party, I received an unexpected call from Pat Masters inviting me to join her and her husband for dinner at the Langam Hotel where they were staying for a few days.

Being such an inquisitive person, I could not resist the kind invitation knowing perfectly well there was something behind it. Anyway, I had nothing to lose and Pauline was just as curious as me. When I arrived, they were waiting in the bar for me where we had a couple of dry martinis before dinner.

The conversation was very general. In fact, they were so easy to talk to it was as if we had been friends for years. Hearing all about Africa was so entertaining and exciting, it really made me think what a dull life I was leading.

It wasn't until we were having our coffee that the blockbuster was dropped on me. Never did I think that I was going to be offered a job in their company. I was completely taken by surprise.

The position was to run one of their camps in which I would be taking over from the South African girl who was going back to Cape Town to be married. If I accepted, they would wish me to start fairly soon so there would be a week with Katia to see how things operated.

Being stunned was to say the least. I had to have time to think about it and get my head round it all, but I only had twenty-four hours as they were leaving for Botswana in one day. They sent me away with so much paraphernalia about Botswana and the camps it wasn't true!

If I decided to take on the job we would meet and final-ise everything before they left London. I was beginning to feel my feet not touching the ground.

In the morning, Pauline and I had a long discussion and no matter how much she wanted me to stay, she thought I would be insane if I didn't take the opportunity of a lifetime, which were my sentiments also.

This would be a totally new chapter of my life. I was a great believer in fate and truly in my soul I felt that meeting them at the party was just destiny.

Pat, David and I had a working breakfast the morning they were leaving and it was from then on I was on in a whirlwind with no time to think about any doubts I may have had.

David had all the right contacts, so would be able to organise a work permit through the Minister of Labour in Gaborone without any problem.

My part in all of this was to start a course of malaria tablets and have one or two vaccinations at the Hospital of Tropical Diseases in London.

Pat wrote me a very handsome company cheque with which I was to buy a list of appropriate clothing from head to toe.

There was a wonderful outfitters of safari clothing just off Bond Street where I was able to buy absolutely everything you could imagine for Africa. I was even able to include a beautiful, soft, suede, long chocolate-coloured skirt and smart boots which Pat had said looked extremely elegant in the evenings, especially as a lot of the female clients dressed rather smart at night as well as during their safari.

I couldn't help but feel guilty in spending so much

money but thought if this was all part of the job then so be it.

'Livingsons', the clothing shop, were so delighted with the fabulous sale that they gave me a wonderful khaki coloured canvas travel bag, seemingly ideal for the planes I would be travelling in as luggage was quite limited.

I couldn't wait to go back to Pauline and show her everything. I felt like Pretty Woman with all the bags, except no Richard Gere waiting for me!

Pauline was a true friend, even if she was disappointed at me going. She was just about as excited as I was of my new adventure.

Gordon and Pauline were actually planning on going to South Africa the following year as it was Gordon's big Five-O birthday and, being a train lover, instead of the Orient Express, which they had done, he longed to go on the famous Blue Train which travelled between Johannesburg and Cape Town. They planned to get Walker and Jones to organise a trip of a lifetime going from Cape Town on the train overnight and flying from Johannesburg up to Maun to continue on to safari, staying in my camp.

It all sounded so incredible, especially when they were now speaking of my camp. I just found it difficult to comprehend at times.

My tickets arrived with quite a great deal of paperwork to fill in for the Botswana authorities, plus a visa and such like.

I contacted my friend from the Embassy in London, Mr Basuti, who was delighted to hear that I was going to be working in Botswana. He had known Pat and David for some time and assured me that they were well respected in the safari business and were good, honest people. He said I was lucky to have this amazing opportunity and if even I needed any help he had obviously many contacts in Botswana. He hoped that when he came over with his family that we may get together. I found this extremely comforting, especially with the thought of living in such a different country on my own and venturing literally into the unknown!

16

My journey was going to be long but I was determined to enjoy every part of it. I flew to London, then on to Johannesburg with South Africa Airways in Business Class which was superb! I had lovely food and wine and plenty of attention, a simply wonderful start to my new career.

My arrival at O.R. Tambo airport was fairly late in the evening, but Pat had booked me to stay overnight at the airport hotel then I was to get the Air Botswana flight first thing early the next morning up to Maun.

I could hardly sleep that night with excitement, longing for morning. It was the same feeling I used to have when I was young and waiting for Christmas Day to arrive.

The airport was huge and incredibly busy. There must have been passengers from every part of the world coming and going, talk about international! This was something else!

After a while I finally found Air Botswana's check in. The girls at the desk were dressed in traditional costume which was so impressive.

From the departure lounge I was able to see the airline's distinctly blue and white colours on the small jet's high-wings. Air Botswana is a busy little carrier, flying to Zambia, Zimbabwe and Kenya, etc. It was just a short flight up to Maun but so interesting to see the landscape changing on the way north.

Maun Airport was so much smaller than I had envisioned, or perhaps it was coming from Johannesburg. Once I went through passport control to baggage reclaim, I immediately saw my name printed on a large board being held by a tall, rugged looking man in his late fifties/early sixties with pure white, short hair. We shook hands and he introduced himself as Jerry Lawson. He was one of Elite Safari's guides who at one time had been a hunting professional with another company in Tanzania but had an accident while hunting, leaving him with a slight limp. He was then approached by Pat and David to join them as a photographic and fishing guide.

Jerry was such a well-known character and the clients thought highly of him. He had such an amazing knowledge of the bush and would entertain them round the camp fire at night with fascinating stories of his experiences. A really totally likeable human being and I think anyone would be privileged to call him a friend.

Outside the airport the dry, hot heat just hit you in the face and you realised just where you were. Jerry threw my bags in the back of a dark green 4x4 jeep with the company's name on the side. I jumped into the front seat beside him and we were off at a high rate of knots. The roads were tarred but the sides were pure sand, with a few donkeys and goats wandering at will. The drive to the office was such an eye opener. I had never in my life seen anything like this. It was impossible to observe all of it.

Jerry was trying to do his best to point out so many things of interest, especially the wonderful African Herero tribal women in their full African dress, walking so elegantly along the side of the road. I was longing for Jerry to stop so I may take a picture of them with my fabulous new camera that Pauline and Gordon had so kindly given me before I left. Unfortunately, the women don't like having their picture taken so that was that.

There was so much for me to learn of African culture that it would take some time. I felt I was bursting with dozens of questions for poor Jerry who was more than happy to help me. He came over as a fatherly kind of person, someone you could really rely on if in need. We arrived at the office which was much larger than I had envisaged. It was a long, one story building with a huge terrace that stretched the length of it, with wonderful huge pots filled with colourful plants.

Pat and David were waiting for me in their office with a jug of ice cold tea which was more than welcome. I also appreciated the enormous ceiling fans burring gently above. Pat assured me that within a short time I would acclimatise myself to the heat.

This was quite an operation at the hub of their company. I was shown the storerooms where all the provisions were kept and flown up to the camps when required. It was almost like Tesco Express! There was every single thing you could imagine to have so no problem cooking first class meals. I was so pleasantly surprised as this was going to make my job just joyous.

After meeting all of the staff and a long session with Pat and David, I felt so much more confident of the job specifications. I had one week with Katia in camp before she left and that surely would be long enough for me to come to terms with it all.

It was also comforting in the fact that Jerry was flying up with me and staying a few days as he would be taking me out into the bush to learn as much as I could of the environment around us, plus the animals that our clients could encounter. The more knowledge I had, the better. So, while Jerry was with me he was my African Encyclopaedia.

Pat organised that my salary would be paid into the Botswana Bank in Maun where my account would be. It certainly would accumulate nicely as I did not see myself spending much money at all. I had a meeting with the bank manager before I flew up to the camp as I did have a little money to invest, which would be a good start.

Jerry took me into town and showed me around so I could get the feel of the place. The little town of Maun had everything you could possibly want. The Riverine trees gave plenty of shade from the burning sun and the main tarred streets were alive with Mercs and brand new 4x4s. I was amazed to see how many safari firms were based in Maun. There were incredible shops selling curios, fabrics, liquor and all the fresh produce imaginable.

Jerry insisted, while we were there, he would make sure I got all the important stuff done. Apart from the bank, I was to register with the doctor and dentist. He was leaving no stone unturned, which I was truly grateful for.

That night I was staying at Pat and David's house, which I was so pleased about as I felt totally exhausted and looked forward to a good night's sleep before heading off the next morning.

Their house was wonderful. It had been built on a colonial style with a huge veranda on the banks of the Thamalakane River, it was all reminiscent of something from *The African Queen*.

We sat on the veranda and sipped our sundowners before dinner. To me, this was heaven and I could literally feel myself falling in love with Africa. There was definitely something magical about it. I couldn't remember ever feeling so relaxed and content. It was as if I had always meant to be here.

The following morning, after a lovely evening with Pat and David who had been so hospitable to me and made me feel like part of the family, I was taken to the office where the small Cessna Twin Turbo Engine plane sat waiting for me. It was then that my stomach turned as I knew this was it. There was no turning back now. I could feel the sheer excitement building up inside me.

The pilot introduced himself and I thought he was rather young, but Jerry informed me that he was one of the best with lots of experience.

My bags were in and lots of provisions were loaded. There was so much, I wondered if the little aircraft would get off the ground. My knees were literally up to my chin as I was squashed between boxes and boxes. Jerry was up front with the pilot and tried to shout a running commentary once we were airborne. It was incredible just how much I was able to see as the plane did not fly high. In fact, they called it tree hopping. Within a short time, I saw springbok running at tremendous speed and also a few zebra. It was truly spectacular. I was actually sorry when Jerry said we were nearly there as I could have taken in several more hours.

Looking ahead of me I saw what looked like just a narrow strip which I was informed was the runway. To begin with I thought they had been joking, but after a few bumps we were tearing along this thing before, thankfully, coming to an abrupt stop. With engines off, the door was quickly opened by an young African man who helped me down. He shook my hand and introduced himself as Jelani which means 'Mighty' in Africaans. He had been born in Botswana and was highly thought of by everyone.

"Welcome to Africa, Ma'am," was all he said with a smile so wide, showing his dazzling white teeth.

We were loaded in to a jeep, bags and all, with a large trailer for the provisions. There was nothing else at this airstrip. It was just surrounded by bush. The terrain was tough, so we literally bounced along past trees and, at times, ducking our heads to avoid low- hung branches and thorn bushes that were almost scratching the side of the jeep.

Only about fifteen minutes passed when I saw Jelani on his intercom speaking in Africaans. Having no idea how long it would take before we reached camp, it was quite a surprise when, literally out of nowhere, the jeep pulled round into a clearing and I started to hear singing and saw Katia and two girls and a boy all standing in line singing the welcome song for me.

My heart was ready to burst. It was impossible to hold back the tears. It was so emotional. It was one of these surreal moments in life, never to be forgotten. I was so honoured, it really did make me feel very special.

The girls were wearing simple khaki dresses with crisp white aprons which had the head of a lion on the front, the company's logo. The boys were just as smart with khaki trousers and t-shirts. Katia greeted me like a long lost friend, with such a warm welcome to 'Chiana Camp' which means 'Place of Rest'. I was then introduced to everyone, including the amazing Jensen, who did some of the cooking. He was so excited to meet me and was looking forward to working with me as he had heard of my culinary skills from Pat. Jensen was a big, gentle giant. He was such a loveable character and the guests were always so fond of him, and now I was here, he certainly could take life a great deal easier.

The camp itself was way beyond my expectations. I never imagined it would be so amazing. My accommodation was a large tent with adjoining shower and loo which had been built from cane and bamboo. It was so wonderful. There was a double bed and a huge oil lamp on the wooden bedside table. A large ebony rail was standing along one side of the tent for hanging clothes. It had plenty of coat hangers, thankfully! Outside my tent was a patio area and two director chairs. What more could anyone want? If this was mine, I was eager to see the guest's accommodation! That would definitely be five star, indeed. Never did I dream of such home comforts in the middle of the bush!

The main lodge was so tastefully furnished with local artisan works with lovely rustic charm. On the walls were incredible pictures of animals and the landscape. There was a most handsome looking dining table with twelve seats and in the corner a half moon bar where, on the top of it, sat a magnificent bronze of an elephant and calf.

The situation of Chiawa was so picturesque, being in the edge of the Delta and with the Mokoro canoes lying there waiting to be used.

One place that I was eager to see which would be my domain was the kitchen area. Jenson was happy to show me what we had to cook with. It was just the basics but literally all that I required, although a far cry from 'Paul's'. Still, I was confident that I would be able to produce my excellent food to impress anyone.

My first evening we were all going to dine together as there were no clients. Jenson was doing a braai as a welcome dinner for me. He loved to get dressed in his black and white checked trousers and tall white hat. He looked so statuesque and had the most infectious laugh I had ever heard. It was easy to see why everyone loved him.

The week was simply superb, with Jelani and Jerry taking turns to take me out into the bush to teach me all that I should know. I was incredibly lucky to see elephants, lions, giraffes and antelopes, and even a pack of wild dogs which looked very scary. The bird life was amazing, so marvellous for photographic enthusiasts with the vibrant colours of the Kingfisher and such like.

I loved every minute of it all and especially out in the Mokoro canoe, gently gliding through the waterways with the stunning water lilies brushing the side of the Mokoro. It had to be the most tranquil feeling I had ever encountered.

Jelani pointed out a few crocodiles sleeping on the banks

and although they looked enormous to me, he said they were quite small ones compared to one crocodile called Pharaoh. Apparently, he was at least twenty feet. Jelani had only spotted him a couple of times and thought he was the most threatening thing he had ever seen.

By the end of the week it was more than obvious why the clients must just love their safari. It had been an experience never ever to be forgotten. I felt so honoured to have seen these wild animals in their own habitat.

If I had to pay for the week's safari I would not have grudged one penny. It was unbelievable that all this was part of my job. How on earth could I have been this lucky! I was totally in seventh heaven. A dream that had come true. At that moment I felt like the luckiest girl in the world.

Pat and David were flying up at the end of the week to see how I had settled in and if I had any problems as the following week we had clients arriving. They were both delighted with a few changes that I had made in the camp, trying to put my own stamp on it.

I cooked a wonderful dinner for them of giant prawns then a delicious goat curry which they found amazing. There was no doubt whatsoever in their minds that Chiawa was in exceptionally capable hands.

17

My first week went like clockwork. The American family with two teenage sons were a pleasure to look after. The boys were not what I expected. They were so polite and very well mannered. In fact, utterly in awe of it all. Having Jerry as their guide was an added bonus for me as we worked so well together. When the Barret family left I felt utter job satisfaction. There was not one singlething that I would have done differently and the feedback from them to Pat had been sensational.

I only had one little incident that no-one knew of which I suppose wasn't bad going! I was awoken one morning with a very strange sensation of something soft crawling slowly up the inside of my leg, almost up to the top of my thigh. My body was coming out in a cold sweat as I gently moved myself out of bed and untied my pyjama bottoms and let them fall to the ground where I spotted an enormous tarantula crawl along the floor. Thankfully, there was a heavy wooden stick by my bed for such happenings which managed to finish off my friend! I felt rather proud of myself that I was able to deal with this and not look like a fool by calling for help. God knows how it got in as I was careful before going to bed, checking for any unwelcome visitors. When I made a joke of it to Jelani, he wasn't so amused and explained that if I had been bitten it may have been fatal, so that took the smile off my face good and proper!

It was David's fiftieth birthday and Pat was having a party for him at 'The Watering Hole' which was a fun bar in Maun. Luckily, I was able to attend as there was a break of a few days before the next crowd arrived. Plus, I wanted to oversee the provisions as I had one dietary request so would be providing gluten free meals for one of the clients and getting Jenson to bake gluten free bread as well.

Upon arriving in Maun, I booked in to the local hotel for a couple of nights as this time I wanted a little freedom, even although Pat and David had offered me a bed.

Mostly everyone from the company, plus a few friends that lived in Maun, had been invited to the party. In fact, Pat had literally taken over the bar for that night. They laid on a buffet and a fabulous band that you really had to dance to. The rhythm was wonderful and it was, all in all, quite the swinging scene.

While dancing with David, I couldn't help notice a couple walking in. The female was a coloured, very tall lady with simply beautiful features and long, back shiny hair to die for. She was just stunning. Her strapless, long red dress looked straight out of Vogue. She was one class act. The only thing wrong with her was the sad expression on her face, or perhaps it was that she obviously did not want to be at the party.

Her partner was much shorter than her, but extremely attractive in a rugged way with a great looking physique. I would have said he was definitely a sports guy.

They joined our table with Pat and David for a short while. He was very arrogant and sure of himself and certainly did not treat this lovely girl with any respect. In fact, he almost ignored her presence. Her name was Mallisa and she had an art gallery in Cape Town. I found her so sweet, but there was certainly a deep unhappiness there which I began to understand. If this was how her boyfriend treated her then she must have been mad, as a beautiful girl like her would have many admirers.

It turned out he was actually one of the Elite Safaris guides. Mark Compton was his name.

For some reason, I felt uncomfortable in his company. He had a strange way of looking at me. It was difficult to tell if the looks were complimentary or not. He asked me for a dance, although I had hoped he wouldn't. I agreed, but as there wasn't much room, we were far too close together, but as his grip was so tight it would have been impossible to push him off without being too obvious. And I was so aware that Mallisa's eyes were on us.

Once they left, I was able to ask Jerry about him. There was something about his character that was trouble with a capital T. Jerry explained that Mark Compton was quite the ladies' man and loved himself, but I had already gathered that. He had been married to a lovely South African lady called Amelia who was much older than he. She owned a winery in Stellenbosch, South Africa, which had been left to her by her first husband when he died. Two years after his death, she met Mark at a friend's party in Cape Town and shortly afterwards they were married.

Mark had a pilot's license so, as a wedding gift, Amelia had bought him a small plane so he could fly between Maun and Cape Town as he had no intention of giving up his job as a guide. He spent most of his time in Botswana, only going back to Amelia every few weeks. Everyone thought it was a strange situation. Occasionally, he would fly Amelia up to Maun where she would a have a few days in one of the camps. However, tragically, on one of their trips the engine seemed to cut off and they had a crash landing into the bushes. Mark was the lucky one with only a broken leg and a few cuts and bruises, but Amelia's neck was broken.

Everyone was totally shocked and stunned as to how the engine had failed as it always had an excellent maintenance check before each flight which Amelia always insisted on for safety.

At the inquest, nothing could be found wrong with the plane, so it was no more than a freak accident or pilot error. But for Jerry and one or two others, the jury was still out!

18

Two days after the party I was back at Chiawa which always felt like going home. We had two couples arriving with one pair being from England. He was in the stock market and they were in Africa for a month starting in Tanzania, Kenya and finishing in Botswana.

The other couple were German and this was their first safari. They were very keen on ornithology, so their guide was to be Harry Owen who was the expert on it, plus he was a wonderful fisherman and was to take the English couple fishing, so all in all, Harry was the right man for all of this.

Unfortunately, poor Harry picked up a sickness bug and was grounded, so Mark was the only guide available at such short notice. Jelani and everyone at camp were so disappointed as Harry was such a popular person whom they respected a great deal.

The atmosphere changed in camp when they found out that Mark was replacing Harry. When I mentioned this to Jelani his reply was simply, "Mr Mark very difficult man to please." Well we will just have to wait and see, I thought.

Before Jelani left to pick up the guests, he put up the wooden plaque that I had bought in a craft shop in Maun. It read 'Enter as strangers and leave as friends', which seemed to just sum up Chiawa.

Once he left, we all got ready for the welcome. I had

learnt the song in Africaans which I was so pleased about.

After a short while, we got our call from Jelani and that was our cue to start singing. I truly loved this little performance, it never failed to excite me. It was worth every bit just to see the expressions of amazement on the clients' faces.

The jeep swung into camp and there we were, lined up, singing our hearts out, Jenson and all. The reaction was just what we wanted. Pure joy!

Margarite Gruner literally dissolved into tears and even the Martins, who had been on safaris before, were clapping their hands with sheer delight. They really did seem very touched as never before had this been done in any camp, so it was truly a first for them.

After the clients had settled into their accommodation, they all gathered in the lodge for lunch. I had made a huge jug of Bloody Mary for them to help themselves to which went down a treat. In the afternoon, Mark was taking them out for the first game drive.

This always gave me peace to set up the table for dinner which would look spectacular with African flowers, candles and bronze animals. The girls in the camp had never seen such presentation. They just loved watching and learning. At that moment in time, I felt so happy! But happiness is like a sunny day … enjoy it while you can!

The evening was a great success with wonderful compliments for my food. What was evident was that there was not one single word of praise from Mark. In fact, I don't think we exchanged words at all. He was an extremely complex man, as if he had a big chip on his shoulder. He certainly was not someone I would choose to be in the company of. I think it was his eyes that bothered me. They looked almost cruel at times.

While I was in the kitchen, I was very aware of Mark standing close behind me. I knew it was him without having to turn round as I recognised his heavy, musky aftershave which was so pungent.

He had come to relay a message from the clients that they would very much like if I joined them for coffee and perhaps a nightcap, but understood if I was too tired, which he said I would be.

I actually was tired and would have been more than happy to decline, but with him almost making my apologies for me, it made me determined to accept their invitation. There was something dark about Mark and his attitude towards women that he comes over as quite chauvinistic. It was almost as if he was jealous of women receiving praise. It was all very strange and I wondered if perhaps he wasn't greatly loved by his parents.

Ever since I had met the Martins, I knew that I had seen them somewhere before, but it was Joyce Martin that recognised me and my canapes from the Walker-Jones part where they actually booked this safari holiday.

We all had coffee and cognacs round the fire and listened to what they had encountered on their drives. However, the whole time I was conscious of Mark's eyes on me which again made me feel a little uncomfortable. Thankfully, over the next couple of months, Jerry and Harry came with the clients, which was just a pleasure with no negative atmosphere at all.

My three month trial was coming to an end and I

couldn't believe how incredibly fast it had passed. Pat had asked me down to Maun for a meeting as it was also end of season for a few weeks and I could take a break, providing that they decided to keep me on. On my way down to the meeting, I thought about how gutted I would be if I didn't stay. I couldn't even contemplate returning to the UK so soon. I felt I would be seen as a total failure and that was not me. Then again, I thought that perhaps I could be too confident and you just never know what is ahead.

Upon arriving in Maun for our meeting, I was rather surprised at just how nervous and anxious I felt. The first thing that caught my eye was a bucket with a bottle of champagne. David asked me to have a seat and then handed me a pen and quite a long document. This was so much more than I had ever anticipated. Not only was my job being secured, but they were offering me a part share of Elite Safaris with a wonderful increase. From time to time my job would involve visiting the other camps and overseeing the culinary side of the operation.

Pat asked me to take my time and read the contract, including the small print with all the legalities, before signing it. I could feel the sheer excitement in me, so much so, that I felt my hand almost shaking when I put my name to the contract. I was now more than a camp manager, I most certainly had proved myself beyond their expecta-tions and the feeling was I had become invaluable to Elite Safaris. How very proud my father would have been. I knew now that I could encourage my mother and George to come out for a holiday as it would possibly be some time before I would go back to the UK for a visit Africa was definitely my future. It felt as if I had been there all my life. It was just the most comforting feeling and I felt so assured that nothing could go wrong with my life there.

That evening, Pat had booked a table at a little restaurant called 'The Duck Inn' for a celebration. She had been so confident that I would accept their terms of employment!

When we arrived at the restaurant we were faced with the sight of Mark literally propping up the bar, extremely intoxicated. David was quite concerned as they had never seen Mark so drunk before. Thankfully, no-one made the suggestion of Mark joining us for dinner as he was no way in a mood for any kind of celebration and that would have been a disaster.

David asked if he could drive him home as he was obviously in no state to drive. Tactfully, David managed to persuade him to be taken home, as by this time he was becoming extremely argumentative as Brian, the owner, was making signs to David to get him out before trouble started.

Pat was obviously concerned as to why he was in this state. The last time he had been like that was after his wife was killed. I took the opportunity to find out why, when his late wife had been so wealthy, was he still working as a guide. Seemingly, to a great surprise, Amelia had left him a very small amount of money while the winery and her total estate were to be sold and the funds to be divided up between several African charities to which she was involved with. Mark had tried desperately to contest the will, but to no avail. The gossip was that, latterly, things between them had been rather acrimonious and that perhaps Amelia had been conscious of Mark's infidelities

19

There was so much of Africa that I wanted to see, so I decided, before starting back at camp, that my short holiday would be in the Cape. My recommendation had been to stay in 'The Bay Hotel' just outside Cape Town where I could swim and enjoy the beautiful beach.

The weather at the Cape was so idyllic and most days were spent at the beach totally chilling out and recharging my batteries. A couple of days before I was due back, it was time to take in the tourist scene and so I got the cable car up Table Mountain which was exhilarating. It was actually quite eerie on the top walking around. The ground looked like something out of Mars while I was almost engulfed in the swirling clouds. Such a strange sensation.

After Table Mountain, I treated myself to a scrumptious lunch of grilled sardines and a cold beer at the waterfront I sat watching the boats and all the activity, feeling life could not get much better and just wondering how different my life would have been if my blood mother had not died and what genes did I have in me from her. I wondered what kind of person I really was!

As I wasn't leaving until evening, I had time to go to the gallery and perhaps Mallisa and I may have a bite of dinner together. Plus, Pat had said it would be an idea if I saw a painting at the right price to buy it for the lodge at camp.

In the evening before I left, I decided to dine in style so

I booked myself a table in their famous sea view restaurant which was located on top of the hotel with awesome views of the bay.

Upon walking into the cocktail bar, I couldn't help notice Mallisa tucked away in a corner with a black gentleman who was heavy set with a shaved head and dark rimmed glasses. Because they were in such a deep conversation that did not look particularly friendly, I thought that perhaps it would be better not to interrupt. I decided that once I had finished my aperitif I would say hello and let Mallisa know that I intended to go to the gallery in the morning.

I tried to keep my eye on them, but it had become extremely difficult to do this as there was now a party of people blocking my view of them. It had only been a short while before the waiter came to take me to my table and it was then, to my disappointment, that I saw they had managed to leave without me seeing them.

There was just something about the whole episode that, for some reason, bothered me and I was angry with myself that I hadn't spoken to her when I first saw them. I even wondered if he may have been her father, but he really didn't look old enough. However, certainly, even after a quick look, he had a face I would not forget.

All through my dinner I felt uneasy as my gut instinct was telling me something was not quite right between them, or was it my mind working overtime as usual!

The next morning, I found the gallery, 'Cape Modern Art', which was near the waterfront. It was in a fashionable area with some snazzy boutiques and bistros.

To my surprise, the gallery was not open. It was well

after opening time, I thought, as everything else was up and running. I wondered if she closed on Mondays like some restaurants do at home. However, as I had no contact number for her, the only thing to do was to get her number when I got back to Maun and suggest that the next time I visited Cape Town we could get together as I definitely planned to return at some point to perhaps do a wine tour when I had more time. There was such a great deal to see and do in South Africa and one week was never long enough.

I was stopping for one night in Johannesburg as in the morning I had a meeting with Anne Gunstburg who was an interior designer and a friend of Pat's.

Annie designed most of her own fabrics and had been commissioned to refurbish two of the camps including Chiawa. Personally, I did not think my camp needed it, but Pat wanted my input in choosing fabrics and soft furnishing which was a lovely compliment. After all, I had never done anything like this before on a professional scale. However, I was really looking forward to it as I always had good taste and an excellent eye for colour.

Annie picked me up from the 'Protea Airport Hotel' where I had stayed and we drove to Santon where her studio was. The premises were like Aladdin's Cave, absolutely everything you could imagine. The colours ranged from subtle to quite exotic in her fabrics. I was so loving picking throws, cushions, lamps and drapes for the guests' accommodation as well as the lodge.

The whole operation started me thinking how much I would love to do this for my own home, and perhaps it was time to consider actually setting down roots and looking at some rather nice little houses just on the outskirts of Maun that had recently been built. After all, it would be wonderful to have my own base when I have time off from camp, I thought. I felt that in my heart Africa was my future. I didn't think it was possible to feel so happy anywhere! Long may it continue, I thought!

When Annie and I had finished our business, she dropped me off at Tambo Airport in just enough time to catch my flight to Maun. While waiting in the queue to check in, I was able to see the passengers come through who had disembarked from the plane that would be taking me up to Maun. It was then I saw Mark which was of no surprise as he often flew down to Johannesburg on business, but no one really knew what business he was involved with as, seemingly, he never discussed his personal life with anyone, not even Pat and David. As far as they were concerned, he did a first class job for them as a guide and that was all that concerned them.

Once I got my boarding pass, I gave one final look in Mark's direction and to my surprise saw him being met by the man that I saw with Mallisa in the bar. There was no mistaking him. I would recognise that face anywhere.

On my way up to Maun, I couldn't help but wonder what involvement Mark had with him. Surely it must be some kind of business, I thought. I doubted very much that he was a friend, but then Mark was a strange soul and I thought he may well have a friend that looked so sinister. As the saying goes, I certainly, for one, would not like to encounter him on a dark night! So my thoughts were that he must know Mallisa through Mark and hopefully not the other way round as he was not the sort of company that I imagined Mallisa would be happy with, which was obvious when I saw them in the bar.

That whole little episode regarding Mallisa still troubled me and I thought I may mention it to Pat and David, even if they thought I was over-reacting.

20

Russell, the Office Manager, met me in Maun and drove me to the office. On arrival, it was very apparent that something was amiss. It was then I got the shock of my life when I was told Mallisa had been found dead.

It took me a minute to actually take in what I had been told, considering I had only seen her two days ago and she looked perfectly healthy.

Seemingly, her girl that cleaned her flat once a week found her lying in her bedroom. It looked as if she had over-dosed on drugs and alcohol which everyone found totally unbelievable as Mallisa was totally abhorrent towards them. As far as alcohol was concerned, she perhaps had a glass of wine occasionally. In fact, from time to time, she actually did volunteer work at the drug rehabilitation centre as her younger brother had died from drugs. Apparently, her brother's death had nearly killed her father, and as she and he were so close, there was no way on earth she would do anything like this to give him such grief once more.

Apart from the shock of it all, I felt quite sick that perhaps I had been one of the last people to have seen Mallisa alive. In my mind, it was now essential that I contact the South African police about seeing her with that man as I really felt so guilty that I hadn't spoken to her that night. No wonder the gallery wasn't open, with Mallisa lying dead in her flat

I even felt ashamed of myself that I had not tried to

contact her that morning, but I think it may have been too late anyway. That I would never know and I would have to live with it.

What really concerned me was Pat and David's reaction when I told them about the bar scene. They were so emphatic that on no account should I get involved with the South African police, especially if the homicide department were brought in. They said that nothing I could do or say would bring Mallisa back and, after all, the only thing that I had seen was a perfectly innocent encounter and I had nothing to prove otherwise. As Pat had rightly said, there would be a post mortem and inquiry. She had almost begged me to let well alone as even being interviewed by the police would be extremely intimidating. It would also involve me having to go back to South Africa and, as my clients were expected in a few days, I had a job to do and so, all in all, I was to try and put it all out of my mind.

In some ways, I could see where they were coming from, trying to protect me, but my instinct was that I may just have been some help to the inquiry. Inwardly, there was a little feeling that if I did pursue this it would definitely jeopardise my job and that was not going to happen at any cost.

With having a day free before heading up to camp, I decided to drive out in my second hand little Toyota pick-up which I just kept at the office. My intention was to view the new development near Boseja, just on the outskirts of Maun. They were small, thatched cottage-style houses with two bedrooms and a large patio area perfect for outdoor cooking. As there were only two left for sale, it was make your mind up time.

Once I had viewed the property, it ticked all of my boxes and I could see myself being extremely content there. I could already imagine having some fun braais with my friends. I decided then to go straight back into Maun to 'Delta Homes' to put down a deposit.

It was a wonderful feeling as I was now a homeowner for the very first time. I just couldn't wait to share my excitement with Pat. She was so thrilled for me and suggested that I had time to see a friend of hers who was a landscaper and did all the work at their home. His business was called 'Gardens for U'.

His name was Steve Prentice, he had worked with his father in Pretoria, but when his father had died, he decided to have a clean break and start up in Botswana. The only family he had was a sister who was a wildlife artist in Cape Town. Seemingly, his mother had died when he was very young.

When I arrived at the cottage, I could see a large pickup with 'Gardens for U' on the side. Standing beside it was a tall, heavyset, fair-haired chap. He had quite a boyish face with a wonderful smile. Not handsome, but there was definitely something attractive about him.

It certainly did not take long for Steve to plan what was required in landscaping. Thankfully, I fully agreed with his ideas and he had even brought some paving stones for me to choose from for the patio area. After we were finished, he persuaded me to have a beer with him before I had to leave.

He was wonderful company and someone I felt so at

ease with. A simply lovely personality. Steve knew nearly everyone in Maun, especially Mark, as he did the landscaping for Mark's house when he and his late wife had it built by the lake where Mark stayed when he wasn't in Cape Town with her. I got the impression that Steve was not a fan of Mark's.

He had met Mallisa a few times and was so saddened to hear of her death, and also found it very questionable as to what really did happen. I was longing to tell him that I had seen her, but thought it was not a good idea as he just seemed to be the sort of person who would definitely act upon it and could stir up a hornet's nest which I did not need.

He gave me a rough date when he thought the work would be finished, which would fit in with my next few days off and hoped that we may have dinner together at his home.

Just before I left for Chiawa, Pat informed me that the coroner's report on Mallisa was death by misadventure and the police had closed the investigation.

21

The plane that flew me up to Chiawa was packed with provisions including some that I had specially requested. There was huge Mozambique tiger prawns, fillets of beef, fresh asparagus and artichokes.

The food for our next guests required a little extra special touch as two of the men ran a well-known restaurant in New York, while the other two were in the construction business.

When I was told that four men would be coming, my mind went into overdrive just wondering what the scene would be until it came to light that two of them were married, but their wives preferred the Bahamas to a safari. The four of them had been friends for many years and once a year would go on an adventure holiday. From shooting the rapids to mountain climbing, even hunting in Canada.

Barry and Ritchie who had the restaurant had been partners for many years, in every sense of the word. They were so totally different from Clive and Gary, but all four got on so well together, it was obvious that they were great buddies. Every single one of them was charming and so well mannered. I could tell instantly that they would be a delight to look after. The only fly in the ointment was that their guide for title days was Mark, which ran a chill through me as I had not seen him since Mallisa died and that was one topic of conversation that would definitely not be brought up. Almost as if it had never happened.

The following days were certainly not what I expected. It was as if Mark had had a lobotomy. Never before had I seen this side of him. He most definitely had a dual personality. It was a delight to be in his company. He was considerate, humorous and so complimentary to my cooking. It was astonishing how bewildered I actually felt, rather like a moth to the flame, as he was so charismatic.

The boys were enjoying their stay at Chiawa so much. The fishing trip had been successful and they had caught a huge bream and wonderful shots of the fish eagle catching its prey.

Barry and Ritchie loved every single morsel that I cooked for them. In fact, they were totally amazed that I had produced Michelin cooking in the bush!

Ritchie was the chef and Barry looked after the business side of things. Ritchie was a little temperamental at times with Barry, which was quite amusing. He always wanted his picture taken at every possible moment until Barry just got the hell in with him. He especially wanted pictures of me and Jenson in the kitchen to take home and put up in his restaurant. I think he would infer that he did some of the cooking in the bush!

On their last evening, I was determined to give them a memorable dinner. I planned to cook tiger prawns and fillet of beef Wellington followed by a huge Baked Alaska. I had chosen some of our best wines from the Cape, a divine Merlot to go with the beef which I knew would be very much appreciated.

My table looked impressive and so did I, as being the

only female at dinner it was time that I really put an effort in. The long, suede, wrap skirt and cream, silk shirt with my sexy little ankle boots looked sensational. Thankfully, there was a little Chanel left, too. Finally, my hair was up and secured with a lovely tortoiseshell comb that I had bought in Cape Town.

The boys had gathered for their pre-dinner aperitifs and savouries and I had made a jug of dry martinis which I was sure the Americans would love. Once Jelani had poured the drinks, it was then I made my appearance to join them.

The looks on their faces were worth every penny of my ensemble. Ritchie, bless him, was the first to clap hands and rush to kiss me on both cheeks saying how incredible I looked. He took a picture of us both which he would head 'Out of Africa'. But what amused me the most was Mark's expression. His jaw literally dropped as he came over and kissed my hand and quietly whispered in my ear, "Sensational."

The evening was a stupendous success. I was on such a high. It had been a long time since I could remember having had such fun. Barry and Ritchie were trying to convince me that I would be a marvellous success in New York and if I ever wanted to open a restaurant there they would give me all the help, as long as it wasn't near them!

We all sat round the fire having coffee and liqueurs. I had never heard so much laughter in sharing stories and jokes before. Everyone was on such good form.

It was getting late and I could actually feel the effect of the wine and as it was an early rise in the morning for me, it was indeed time to let the boys finish the malt that they were savouring so much. So, feeling pleasantly mellow and tired, I retreated to bed.

I lay there listening to the chatter and laughter for a short while before I heard the 'good nights' shouted to each other, followed by the total silence of the night

As I was starting to drift off to sleep, it was then that I became aware of something outside my tent. Lying perfectly still, I was imagining a hyena prowling around looking for food as this often happened. That was why I was so careful not to leave anything around in the kitchen.

It was such a shock when I heard the zip of the tent being opened slowly, at once my body froze and my heart was pounding. I was about to scream, but then it became apparent to me who was coming in. There was no mistaking the pungent aftershave.

The zip was then gently pulled back up and it was as if a switch had been turned off in my mind, wiping out all sense of right and wrong. I knew exactly what was going to happen and I had no intention of stopping it. The feeling of desire and sheer lust was just beyond my control. More than anything at that moment, I needed and longed for Mark to make love to me. At any cost, my sensuality was on fire and there was utterly no turning back now. No matter how much I knew I would regret it.

Not one word was uttered between us as I lay there hearing the thud of his heavy belt as his trousers hit the floor. So gently he slid into bed and slowly started to undress me. My heart was pounding almost out of control with utter anticipation. His hands were strong yet felt so soft as he explored my body. We made love all night until just before dawn and just as quietly, with still not a word between us, he left as daylight arrived.

I lay wishing it had just been a dream, but the way my body felt, it was no dream. In the cold light of day, I could not believe what I had let happen. There was no love in our feelings at all, simply animal instincts. I had got what I needed and had literally used him, which didn't concern me. My only worry was what the repercussions might be, knowing what a bastard he was. I could only hope Pat and David would never find out and if they did, I would deny it.

For me, it was business as usual, but the thought of coming face-to-face with Mark at breakfast was just a little daunting to say the least.

I was up and out first and working in the kitchen with Jenson when the boys all appeared, some looking a bit bleary-eyed! They were nearly finished their cooked breakfast and enjoying plenty of strong, black coffee when a very tired Mark made an appearance, apologising for being late as he could not sleep last night and as he didn't have his sleeping pills with him.

We both avoided eye contact, in fact, he only spoke to the boys and Jelani regarding when they would leave which was, for me, the sooner the better as I felt extremely uncomfortable in his company.

I only wished that I may never clap eyes on him again, but that was impossible, so I thought I must live with my mistake and only hoped that in time, I could erase it from my mind, which I knew would be difficult as every time I had to see Mark would be a constant reminder. Almost a punishment.

When Jelani returned from taking the guests and Mark to the plane, I was sitting on my own enjoying a pot of coffee. I asked Jelani to come and join me as I felt the need for general conversation on how well the safari had gone. We sat and digested the last few days and how much he had enjoyed the men's company on safari. The only thing for him to spoil it was that Mark was the guide. When I asked him why, it was then he told me he hated "Mr Mark" and that he was a very bad person which didn't surprise me, but that only made me feel worse than I already did.

It had been nearly four years ago that one of the local girls from Maun called Leoni worked at Chiawa. Jelani and she had fallen in love, but knew how careful they had to be as if their relationship was discovered one, or both, of them would lose their job. Unfortunately, Mark became aware of their love for each other and Leoni was dismissed. The sad thing was that Leoni was pregnant and no matter how much Jelania begged her father to agree to them marrying, he was adamant that she would be sent away to have the baby and Jelani would never see her or the child again. Her father worked with the church in Maun and felt that she had shamed the family.

This totally broke Jelani's heart and, to this day, he has no idea where Leoni and his child are. It was more than likely that the baby would be adopted by now.

22

In the following weeks we were booked solid, so when I finally had some breathing space, I just couldn't wait to see my home.

Steve Prentice had been so helpful, sending me pictures from time to time as the house developed. From what I had managed to see, his work looked just what I wanted. I felt so excited thinking of all the things I had to do and get for it.

The local furnishing that I had ordered were all ready for me, including a handsome dining table made out of sleepers.

My soft furnishings were being sent up by Annie, my interior designer friend from Johannesburg. They were to be included in everything for the camp.

Annie was wonderful as when I contacted her about the house and explained that there was no way I would manage a trip to Johannesburg to choose what I wanted, we simply discussed what I had in mind and, if I was happy to trust her, she would see to it all.

When I drove out to the house, I could see Steve working on the flagstones and a couple of workmen were finishing the kitchen and bathroom. It definitely would not be long before I would be able to move in.

Steve had brought huge clay tubs for my approval which would be planted with easy care plants and shrubs to sit on the patio. When he was finished, I kept my promise and let him take me for lunch. He was such good company to be with and I loved his enthusiasm over my garden and house.

There was just one very uncomfortable moment while enjoying lunch when he told me that Katrina and Mallisa had been friends and Mallisa often sold some of Katrina's painting in the gallery. His sister hated Mark for the way he treated Mallisa at times. He seemed to have such a cruel streak in him and God help any woman that had anything to do with him. As far as Steve was concerned, it was 'the kiss of death'.

I could feel my colour change and only hoped Steve thought it was because it was such a hot day. God knows what this decent guy would think if I were to tell him what I had done.

If we were to be friends, something I knew I would very much like, I would hate him to lose respect for me. I knew that if I opened my mouth that was sure to happen, as right then I didn't have much respect for myself.

In the next few weeks I was able to fly down once or twice before moving in to the house and on each occasion most of my time was being spent with Steve. It just seemed the natural thing to do and I was finding myself really looking forward to his company. There was not one single thing questionable about Steve.

It was becoming quite apparent that his feelings towards me were more than just good friends and the friendship may very well turn into something else.

It was a lovely thought that this may be a sustainable relationship, but I certainly needed time as I could not bear to make another mistake.

Finally, a couple of weeks later, I moved in to the house with Steve's help. It really made things so much easier for me. We scrubbed floors, placed the furniture, hung the drapes and unpacked all the kitchenware that I bought.

By the time we were finished making it as comfortable as possible, both of us were exhausted. Steve still had final touches to do outside which looked amazing. I was so ecstatic about how everything looked that I started thinking about a house-warming party.

I was happy to go to the supermarket and buy some steaks for us that evening, but knowing how tired I was, Steve had booked a table at The Duck Inn.

Our evening was simply brilliant. We never stopped talking and laughing and with good food and wine it had to be the perfect combination. After dinner, we drove home and before Steve left, he asked me to open his house-warming gift to me.

When I unwrapped it, I literally could not believe my eyes in seeing the most wonderful painting of a pride of lions by Keith Joubert, a famous artist from Africa. My first instinct was that it was far too much for me to accept to which he replied, "You cannot refuse a gift given from the heart." There was no answer to that and he hung the painting on the wall. It looked incredible, as if it had always been there.

As he was leaving he turned, as I thought, to kiss me goodbye on my cheek, but this time he held my face and kissed my mouth so slowly that it sent an electric shock through me. In an instant, he was gone and I was left almost reeling. I was so disappointed that he left, but I could tell Steve was not a one-night stand person and perhaps he was the first man to show me great respect. I was sure he would know when the time was right for us.

The next morning, Steve arrived with more security locks for the house and it was going to be left empty when I was in Chiawa. Although, he was going to check on it nearly every day as his landscaping business was quite nearby.

I had already got another set of keys for him, knowing they would be in safe hands and I could have peace of mind.

While we were having coffee, he presented me with a smallish flat shaped box and declared it was something he just wanted me to have. On opening the box, I could see it was lined in pink satin and nestling among the satin, much to my surprise, was a little revolver.

Before I lifted it out, Steve explained that it had belonged to his late mother and, thankfully, she never had to use it, but it always made his father feel more at ease when he left her to go on business.

It was a lady's gun called a Nighthawk 1911 with a small frame and a much thinner grip with single action. All of this meant absolutely nothing to me.

He felt as his father had, but in my case, not only to have it here with me in the house. I was to take it with me to the camp as, no matter how safe I felt with Jelani and company, it was better to have my own protection for any circumstance that may arise.

When I thought about it, I supposed he was right as

there were stories of poachers getting a bit too close to some camps.

Before I was to leave, he gave me lessons with the gun. I was rather pleased with myself at what a good eye I had and within no time, I felt quite confident with it.

Steve had thought of everything. He even had the license renewed in my name just to keep things right. I couldn't help but think what on earth my mother would think of her daughter travelling around with a Nighthawk in her bag!I could hardly believe it myself. I felt as if I was starring in a Bond movie, or something! It was actually laughable, except that I knew Steve took it seriously.

In a way, it did give me a feeling of security and some comfort. I just hoped I would never have to use it, but in Africa, you never knew what may happen.

Back in camp, we were preparing for our next group arriving. We had a mother and daughter from Ohio and a couple from England. Their guide, of course, was Mark, but it now did not bother me one little bit. He had been in the camp a couple of times since the incident, if I may call it that.

His attitude and manner towards me was just what I expected and it really was perfect for me. We hardly spoke at all and only when necessary. In fact, we treated each other with contempt which suited me perfectly! I really felt Mark was absolutely disdainful and hated being in his very presence.

My mind started thinking that it would not surprise me that Mark may, in some way, had been responsible for Mallisa's death. But how? The only possible reason could be that she knew something that lead to her demise.

Even if Mark had a foolproof alibi as he had still been in Maun when it had happened. It was the day after her death that I saw him meet his friend in Johannesburg.

23

Our guests arrived and instantly I was aware that the next few days were going to be rather interesting.

Dr and Mrs Crawford were a delightful couple whom had never been to Africa before and it had been a lifelong dream of theirs. He had just retired and a safari was on their must-do list. Dr Crawford's hobby was photography, so he could not have come to a more suitable place for it.

On the other hand, we had Mrs Wilkinson and her daughter, Emma-Louise, who had a touch of the 'Barbie Doll' about her! I would say she was late teens and very aware of her fantastic body. If her top had been any tighter she would have needed oxygen! Unfortunately, she had one of those high-pitched, childish, America voices that grated on ones nerves, plus an almost hysterical laugh. The thought of it for the next few days was charming! I just hoped that when she went out into the bush that Mark would be able to shut her up, or no-one would ever see any animals!

That evening over dinner, Mrs Wilkinson never stopped talking. It was evident she had a problem with nerves, or such like. The poor Crawfords never got a word in edge-ways, even when I desperately tried to bring them into the conversation.

It all poured out of Mrs Wilkinson regarding her life history. She had been divorced for two years from her second husband, Tony Miller. Seemingly, Mr Wilkinson had died suddenly.

She and her daughter had a beauty spa in Delaware which explained a few things to me as I was aware that Mrs Wilkinson had had a few nip-and-tucks! Nevertheless, she was in good shape for her age.

As the evening progressed, it was so obvious that Emma-Louise had become rather infatuated with Mark which gave me much amusement. You would have had to be blind not to see what was developing between them as he was reciprocating big time to her.

Even Jelani would look at me and shake his head in a funny, disapproving way which I hoped Mark did not see. The only person who seemed oblivious to it all was her mother, or perhaps this was because she had seen it all many times before.

I got the feeling, even just over dinner, that whatever Emma-Louise wanted she got. And Mark would most certainly come under that category. I just hoped it would not end in tears, especially in the camp.

In the morning, the two parties were to be split up. Dr and Mrs Crawford were going with Jelani on the Mokoro through the Delta and the Wilkinsons on a drive with Mark.

As the Crawfords would be back for lunch, I only had to prepare a picnic for the Wilkinsons as they would be out until afternoon.

As everyone was getting ready for the day's adventure, Mrs Wilkinson came to me and declared that she felt unwell with a migraine and would have to go back to bed. It was then that Mark requested a bottle of champagne to be included in the cool box along with the beers and water. Someone was going to have a rather nice sundowner.

Emma-Louise was almost beside herself with excitement at the prospect of having Mark all to herself. I think her mother's migraine was a gift from heaven.

Later in the day, I decided to take some camomile tea to Mrs Wilkinson and see if she was feeling any better. When I entered the tent, I was pleased to see her sitting up and looking more like herself. At least she had her colour back as in the morning the poor soul was as white as a sheet.

She was extremely grateful that I had brought her tea and a little food. When I went back to collect the plates, she was sitting on her patio looking rather vulnerable and for some reason I felt sorry for her. She looked so different without any makeup on and her hair pulled back from her face which drew my attention to the dark shadows under her eyes.

The one thing that I felt she needed was a little company when she asked me if I wasn't too busy would I sit with her for a while. It has never failed to surprise me how people will open up to virtual strangers about their private life.

Emma-Louise had taken the death of her father very badly. She had been the apple of his eye, so after he died, Mrs Wilkinson admitted that she spoilt her rotten trying to compensate for the loss of her father, but it had obviously been the wrong thing to do and she just prayed that one day Emma-Louise would find a decent boyfriend as, so far, some of the friendships that she had were a little unsuitable.

It did cross my mind that she would be in a very different league with Mark.

Mrs Wilkinson's late husband had a sailing boat in the Delaware Bay where he and Emma-Louise would go most weekends and sail. It was one of these afternoons on the boat that her father had a heart attack. Emma-Louise was a good sailor and managed to get the boat back on her own, but sadly her father had already died before the paramedics got to him. I really was sorry for Emma-Louise as she must have felt like I did when I lost my father unexpectedly, it certainly leaves a massive void in your life and perhaps a little chip on the shoulder that you have been unfairly cheated out of many years in your life with him. Never to see you married and enjoy grandchildren, plus a million other things that you would share with your father.

It was two years later that Mrs Wilkinson met Tony Miller, a lieutenant in the Delaware Police Department at a fundraising event for charity. He had literally swept her off her feet and within a short time they were married. He was much younger than her and was quite a party animal. Much against Emma-Louise and close friends' advice, she refused to listen to anyone and they were married at the registrar's in Ohio.

Barely a year went by after their marriage that Emma-Louise found out he was having an affair with one of the beautiful Thai beauty therapists at their spa. Emma-Louise, although feeling sorry for her mother, was actually delighted that she had caught him out as she detested him and hated the way he seemed to use her mother.

The three of them living together had been hell on earth

for Mrs Wilkinson, with constant arguing between Tony and Emma-Louise, almost to the point of her mother nearly having a nervous breakdown with trying desperately to keep the peace. Within months, the divorce was through as Tony could not contend it.

Emma-Louise had been suspicious of him, so she had hired a private investigator to have him watched and within a couple of weeks he was caught red-handed with the therapist one afternoon at her flat.

No wonder Mrs Wilkinson had a nervous disposition. Emma-Louise was definitely a handful! She sold the house and bought a smart new build in Pine Creek in Delaware so that she and Emma-Louise could have a fresh start. It turned out this holiday was supposed to be a healing process for Mrs Wilkinson after the divorce.

The Crawford's loved the morning in Mokoro and by the time their day was finished, Dr Crawford had managed to get a fantastic photo of a pack of wild dogs round their den. There hadn't been many guests who had shown such enthusiasm and it was such a pleasure to see.

The sun had gone down and it was getting way past the time Mark should have returned, even taking into consideration he had planned the champagne for sundowners at the elephant watering hole.

Emma-Louise was certainly not clad for an evening drive, having not taken my advice to wear a warm jacket. By now, she would be extremely cold, to say the least.

As the time went on and Mrs Wilkinson and the Crawfords met for pre-dinner drinks, I could see how anxious she had become, so I tried to reassure her that

Emma-Louise would be quite safe and that Mark was a very capable guide. Plus the fact, if there had been any kind of problem, he would have radioed in to Jelani. However, by now Jelani was looking more and more concerned for Emma-Louise. After all, she was our responsibility.

Jelani told me he tried to contact Mark with no success and that he was going out himself to see if he could find them before it got any later. But, by the grace of God, I saw the headlights of the jeep roaring into camp. I think every single one of us sighed with relief, especially Mrs Wilkinson who by now was on her second gin and tonic.

Mark, being as arrogant as usual, made no apologies or gave any reasons for why they were so worryingly late. It was difficult not to take my eyes off Emma-Louise, as it looked as if she had been dragged through the bushes backwards. Her clothing was simply filthy and her shorts were torn. I had never seen any client come back in this mess, a little dusty perhaps, but this was a different ball game.

Even her mother looked shocked at her appearance and for the first time, Mrs Wilkinson's tone towards her daughter was very different as it was impossible to ignore the raised voices from their tent.

All evening, Mark had a smug expression on his face which for anything I would have loved to have wiped off. It was so blatantly obvious to one and all what had taken place on the safari as Emma-Louise was all over Mark like a rash, which was getting rather embarrassing for the Crawfords. As for her mother, she had got stuck into the gin which helped her to turn a blind eye.

No doubt by that stage, Mark would have been told the family history and I wondered if she had been stupid enough to tell him that, once she becomes twenty-one, she will inherit a large amount of money that her father had put in a trust for her. He did this when he sold the pharmaceutical company, not long before he died. It was shortly after his death that her mother had bought the beauty spa purely as fun to keep Emma-Louise happy. Therefore, nothing would surprise me if Emma-Louise became Mark's next acquisition. God help Mrs Wilkinson if that was to be.

In the morning, I could hear Mrs Wilkinson questioning Emma-Louise that her bed in their tent had not been slept in. It certainly did not need wondering where she had slept. She was a pretty brave girl to go wandering through the night, even if she did have a torch. Anything could have happened to her. I only hoped it was worth it.

I found it sickening to see how pleased Mark was with himself, especially when I heard him bragging to everyone that Mrs Wilkinson and Emma-Louise had invited him to Delaware for Christmas, to which Emma-Louise was beside herself with excitement. So my intuition had been correct, Mark definitely had Emma-Louise as his next conquest. God her help, I thought.

After Jelani had taken our guests and Mark to the airstrip, he came to me rather anxious that I should have warned Mrs Wilkinson about Mark. Jelani had found Mrs Wilkinson to be a kind and gentle lady who did not deserve Mark involved in any way with her life as no good would come out of it. In fact, another tragedy would happen. That was for sure.

I tried to explain to Jelani that it would have been wrong for me to say that Mark was totally undesirable as I did not have one piece of evidence to prove he had anything to do with deliberately causing the crash that killed his wife, or the death of Mallisa. It was all purely circumstantial. Thankfully, he did try and understand, but of course I could not tell him one of the main reasons being if Mark and Emma-Louise had an argument and it came out that I had said anything detrimental about him he most definitely would say it was pure jealousy on my part as he wanted nothing to do with me after sleeping with me. Then the whole sordid mistake would be out.

I think it was only then that I really comprehended what Mark had over me. I would do anything to keep my secret safe from Steve as how could he ever respect me again, especially as it was with Mark of all people.

And, just to add to my horror, Jelani was surprised that no one in the company had mentioned that Mark was accused of rape, but that Pat and David put him in touch with a brilliant lawyer in Gabarone, who defended him, and Mark was found not guilty.

It had not been long after he was married to Amelia when she was in the Cape and he would stay most weeks on his own at the house on the lake in Maun. Amelia had hired a very pretty, young, coloured girl to come in once a week and clean the house and do Mark's laundry.

He had come back one afternoon from a particularly boozy lunch with friends at The Duck Inn and found the girl still working. Her story was when he made advances to her and she refused him, he then became almost violent and out of control and she just did not have the strength to fight him off. But it was purely his word against hers that she had had sex without consent.

Mark's lawyer had made a mockery out of the case and the prosecution lawyer was not in the same league as Mark's. Amelia had threatened to divorce him, but unfortunately Mark somehow managed to get another chance. But Jelani said things between them were obviously never the same when she would come up to Chiawa.

By now, I was feeling physically sick at what I had allowed to happen to myself. Why in the name of hell was I never told all this when I started working at Elite Safaris? There would have been no way that I would have allowed that bastard near me. I actually felt quite tainted by it. At that moment, I could have quite easily murdered Mark without a second thought.

I knew that what happened between us was one secret I would have to take to my grave.

I am sure we are all entitled to one mistake in our lives, some worse than others, where our punishment is to live with it for the rest of one's life.

24

It was a most welcome break from the camp as I was feeling tired having been working full on for weeks. So the prospect of Steve and my own home for a few days was a comforting thought.

When I arrived in Maun, Steve was waiting for me to take me to the house.

Being with him was the most wonderful, comforting and secure feeling I had ever felt. Not even in the good days with Tony did I feel so secure. There was always an uncertainty about us.

It was realising what it was really like for someone to absolutely love you. How unselfish they are in always putting you first and feeling like you are the most important thing in their life.

It would have been impossible for me not to have fallen in love with Steve and I felt the luckiest girl ever to have found him.

I was almost frightened of feeling so happy, as happiness and I, at times, did not go hand in hand.

In a short space of time, the house looked so much more established because of the shrubs and colourful plants that had grown. Back in the UK, this would have taken months. But in Africa, it was almost instant.

Inside, Steve had filled a huge vase with dozens of beautiful gold roses to welcome me home that gave a heavenly sent throughout the house.

I almost had to pinch myself that he was for real.

We both decided that this break was the ideal time to have a small house-warming party. Nothing elaborate. Purely champagne and canapes for a couple of hours . The last thing I wanted was to spend my short holiday cooking for friends. This was definitely not a busman's holiday.

The party was great fun. Everyone knew each other, as they were mostly from the company which included a couple of our pilots and their girlfriends.

Pat and David brought me a wonderful, large, wooden hippo with its baby that just looked so in keeping with my house.

In fact, the house warming gifts were almost embarrassing. Everyone had been far too generous. There was simply nothing that I did not care for.

After the party, Steve and I had a simple supper with a bottle of Pinotage which we enjoyed sitting out on the patio while Steve admired his work.

That evening, I hoped beyond hope that this time he would not leave. Thankfully, my hopes were granted and it was then he told me how much in love he was with me. He managed to take a couple of days off work, so before I had to go back up to Chiawa we were never apart. And I felt the more I was with him, the more I loved him.

It was the first time that I felt as if I would be content to stay in Maun. Up until then, I just couldn't wait to go back up. How amazing it is that, when you are in love, you no longer think as a single person. I was beginning to feel as if I would be leaving half of me behind with Steve and trying desperately to work out when I would be able to come back next.

Steve had asked me to marry him, but it would only be when the time was right for me to feel and know that I was finished with Elite Safaris.

Steve's future plans, which now included me, were that when he wished to retire, he would sell his landscaping firm. As he never wanted to settle in Maun for the rest of his life, we would travel the world to see where we would like to spend the rest of our lives together. As the song goes, we have all the time in the world, but at this moment in time, it's one step at a time.

Steve made me promise that on one of my few days off from camp that we would fly down to Johannesburg where a friend of his late father's had a jewellers shop and I could choose a ring of my choice. It was where his mother got her pearls and pieces of jewellery which, when she died, his sister rightly so inherited them.

The family home, where Steve had always lived, was a large colonial style with, as to be expected, wonderful gardens so beautifully manicured, just an abundance of colour. Inside needed some decorating, which Steve wanted me to totally take care of. I had only been in his home a couple of times and realised how beautiful it could be. I certainly would be very proud to have it as my home.

Steve had wondered, when the time came, where I would like to be married and if it would be Scotland or South Africa where we would get wed in the garden and have a huge marquee for the reception. In my mind, there was no question. I couldn't think of anything more lovely and romantic to have our wedding in his home.

There was no doubt in my mind that mother and George would come, as well as Pauline and Gordon as they were the ones from the UK that really mattered. The majority of guests would be from Africa, anyway. I could hardly believe that I was actually thinking of a wedding sometime.

I knew how much my mother would love Steve. He was everything she would have wished for me as well as in a son-in-law. I longed for her to meet him so I was able to show him off as I was desperately proud of him. He was indeed the most decent and respected man, apart from my father, I had ever met and I knew I would be so honoured to be his wife.

25

On arriving back in camp I was bursting to tell Jelani and Jenson my incredible news and, just as I expected, they were so happy for me. Pat and David were too, except they hoped that I would be staying with Elite Safaris for some time which I assured them I would be, they were about to celebrate twenty-five years of marriage.

The silver wedding party was being held on the island of Namaserie, which was often used by the company, especially for bird watching and marvellous fishing. It was such a picturesque setting, almost magical, or something out of a wildlife film.

There were little bungalows scattered through it. Just so tastefully built and utterly in keeping with the habitat.

The party would be about forty or so, which for me, with Jenson's help, was no problem. As there would not be enough accommodation in the bungalows, most of the younger guests would bring their own tents, which was seemingly the norm at parties in Africa.

The plan was that the guests flew into Chiawa in the company planes and then travel by motorboat over to the island. Seemingly, one couple had their own little plane which they used to go from Johannesburg to Maun from time to time.

There was great excitement building up towards the party which was most definitely going to be a new challenge for me, which I would love.

The only disappointment for me was that Steve, who had been invited, unfortunately wasn't going to be there. He had to fly down to Gabarone to a very important meeting at Government House as he had got the contract to landscape a new government building in Maun which was going to be extremely lucrative for him.

In a way, it may have been for the best as I don't believe in mixing business with pleasure and possibly would not have the time to enjoy ourselves together.

The party was to be a huge success for Pat and David, which they rightly deserved.

My first task was making the anniversary cake which was going to be an African theme, something that no one would have seen anything like anywhere. It was to be a total work of art.

I started making miniature marzipan animals and replicas of acacia trees with their yellow and white flowers. My rondavels were going to be made out of matchsticks and grasses for thatched roofs and I had ground almond, so they actually looked like fine sand. The cake was pure genius on my part.

Once it was finished and I finally let Jelani and Jenson see it, they were totally mesmerised at the intricate detail of the work I had put into it. I knew Pat and David would be utterly thrilled with it. In fact, it was a sacrifice to cut it!

Foodwise, we were having a huge spit with a pig, plus a wonderful buffet. All the wines and champagne were coming from the Cape. David had sent two of the boys from the office in a truck to drive down and pick up the wines.

I was simply in my element organising the party. Africa had changed me and I was so much more confident and assertive than I had ever been. I also felt that the experience in Morocco had made me much harder as a person that never again would I ever allow myself to be hurt and make such an inconceivable misjudgement of someone. A hard lesson indeed which, thankfully, would never be repeated. I expect it's all part of making us who we are and able to cherish the feeling of trust and appreciate when life is good for as long as it can be. As my father used to say, no one knows what's behind that corner.

It took myself and Jelani, with the help of a couple of the girls from the camp, several journeys back and forth with provisions and setting the party up.

The plan was for everyone to dine outside, so we had lots of tables with a lantern on each, as well as all other huge ones on the island. When every one of them was lit it was simply spectacular. The whole effect was so beautiful.

It took some time before we were all finished and satisfied that everything was just perfect, we had even put tiny lights amongst the trees which were magical.

I knew Pat and David would be so impressed, as would all of the guests. I could not have done more if I had tried. Seeing their faces when they arrived on the island would be my thanks.

Jenson spent hours rubbing the pig with salt and a special spice mix of his own which he liked to do almost twenty-four hours before putting it on the spit. The aroma was going to be out of this world.

We all got back to camp feeling fairly exhausted and

looking forward to a quiet, early night and a simple supper so we would be in good shape for the party. But to my disappointment, Jelani informed me that at some time that evening, Mark would be coming into camp a day ahead of the party. Jelani surmised that it must have been one of Mark's rather mysterious trips that he ventured on about once a year, but only when there were no guests in camp and he was not working as a guide. It always seemed to be at this time of year, which was late summer.

Jelani once innocently asked Mark where he could have possibly been to get the jeep in such a filthy state, which poor Jelani had to wash down. But he was told, in no uncertain terms, that it was none of his or anyone's business and if Jelani knew what was good for him, he would not open his mouth regarding a private matter which only concerned Mark.

In fact, Jelani's feelings were that the less he knew of Mark's business, the better it was for him. Jelani only told me as he felt he was able to trust me which was so right, as I felt the same. I didn't want to even imagine what Mark could be up to. Whatever it was, it would be trouble and most certainly not my concern.

For our supper, I made a huge pizza that Jenson and Jelani really enjoyed so much. It was amazing so authentic as we cooked it in our large clay oven.

The girls had set the table and were always so excited when there were no guests in camp as we were all able to dine together. I had opened a bottle of wine for myself as neither Jenson nor Jelani drank alcohol. But I felt in need of a glass after the work I had put in for the party. The last item to take over had been the cake and it was safely stored away, so I was well and truly ready to simply relax for the evening. It was that wonderful feeling when all the hard graft is done and one can sit back and, in a strange way, enjoy being so tired, but satisfied.

We had just finished our supper when the jeep appeared and, just as Jelani had predicted, it was in a shocking mess. It actually looked as if he had been in the Dakar Rally. There was dry mud and sand everywhere. When Mark got out of the jeep he didn't look much better and it was obvious to see he was in one of his dark moods.

Jelani literally dropped everything he was doing to immediately clean the jeep, even without one word from Mark.

It was a routine that must have been performed many times without a please or thank you.

When Jelani was finished, the jeep looked as if it had come straight out of the showroom. It was difficult to believe it was the same vehicle.

Much to my relief, Mark requested, through Jelani, that he wished for a bottle of scotch and supper brought to his tent as he was extremely tired and had some work to do and wished not be disturbed that evening. It suited me and everyone else perfectly, as none of us wanted to spend any time with him, especially when he was in that kind of frame of mind.

I rustled up a salad with some leftover pizza for him which Jelani took up to him. However, as I was going to be passing his tent anyway, I told Jelani that I would drop off the Johnny Walker whisky so that he may give Jenson a hand in cleaning up the kitchen, which was always a tiresome job.

As I approached Mark's tent, I was able to hear him starting the shower, so thankfully would be able to leave the whisky in the tent without having the pleasure of seeing or speaking to him.

Before I entered the tent, I called out his name, just to make sure he was actually in the shower and as there was no answer, I ventured in and placed the bottle on the table.

As I turned to leave, my foot caught his broad, leather belt that he always wore. It was lying over the chair and hanging down to the floor, half covered by his shirt. But what my eye was drawn to was a small, brown, suede looking type of pouch tucked inside the lining of his belt. It looked similar to a poacher's pocket.

While still hearing the shower running, aware that I only had a couple of minutes at most, I had the pouch in my hand without even thinking. With my heart racing like mad, I quickly opened the draw strings and emptied the contents into the palm of my hand.

By now, I felt as if my heart was going to explode out of my chest when the strange cloudy looking stones fell out. Knowing perfectly well what they were, I hurriedly put them back and quickly placed the pouch into the belt as I suddenly became aware of silence and knew he must be out of the shower.

But to my absolute horror I saw one of the stones on the floor which must have slipped through my fingers. Not surprising as my hands had been shaking so much.

I knew there was absolutely no time to put the stone

back, so I grabbed it and fled out of his tent, trying desperately to control my breathing.

Thankfully, no one was around as I would have found it impossible to speak without trying to gasp for air. My body was literally trembling from head to toe as I imagined the consequences if Mark had caught me.

Back in my tent, I sat on my bed just staring at the uncut diamond in front of me. I had no idea how much the stone would be worth once cut, but altogether in the pouch I knew there must have been an incredible value of diamonds.

I felt so sick at having this stolen item in my possession and all I could think was how on earth I was going to get it back before he noticed it was missing. Surely he would have every damn one counted and weighed. I just prayed he didn't check them every five minutes, for my sake.

It was impossible to believe how, in a matter of minutes, you feel as if your life has been changed. I finally knew what Mark's mystery trips were about.

There had been an article in one of the papers that blood, or conflict, diamonds, as they were referred to, were being trafficked from the mines in Botswana then passed on to a dealer for vast amounts of money. It was some little pension that Mark was stacking away for himself.

It would not have surprised me if he had a bank account in Switzerland, or the likes, to secure his money safely. Possibly not even in his own name.

Once I had calmed down, I had to really make a plan to get the stone out of my possession without being able to tell Jelani, or, in fact, any living soul. It was totally my nightmare alone as I would never have put Jelani in danger, no matter how much I knew that he would do this for me and replace it.

There was no doubt in my mind that it may well be the reason for Mallisa's death. Even if Mark himself did not physically do it, he most certainly was involved in orchestrating it. To me, he was nothing but a cold-blooded murderer who would stop at nothing for his illegal gains.

I felt shocked at myself that, for a moment, I began to actually wonder what would happen if I kept the diamond. But I knew that even if I did get away with it, how could I take it to a respectable jewellers to have it cut without questions being asked which would, of course, have to involve Steve as he most certainly would want to know where I had acquired it. And then to be made out a thief would make me no better than Mark. I knew it would most definitely be the end to a wonderful relationship which was inconceivable and unthinkable. This was madness and there was no question it had to be returned.

Why on earth would anyone in their right mind brand themselves a thief for the rest of their life for something purely material? Every time they looked at the diamond it would merely be a constant reminder of the dishonesty, to say the least.

There were so many ramifications to the situation that I found myself in. If ever I needed sound advice it was then. But there was no one I could turn to and involve. I was totally on my own.

Even the thoughts of informing the Maun police simply terrified me in case, in some bizarre way, I incriminated myself as Mark would stop at nothing. I knew it would only be my word against his that I was in no way involved with the diamonds.

26

That night, I was unable to sleep for thinking how I would get the diamond back and get myself out of the mess that, once again, I seemed to have got into. This one was a corker. With such a dire outcome.

There was no way that, during the day, I could even attempt to replace it as Mark wore his belt all the time. My only possible hope was once he had gone to bed after the party and, if he ran true to form, he would hopefully be so inebriated that an elephant could enter his tent and he wouldn't notice. I knew that would be my only chance and I hoped to God he did not count the diamonds before that.

Thankfully, Mark was taking his own mobile tent that he took to parties and events if there was no accommodation for him. I knew this would make my task that little bit easier to achieve as if he was to stay in one of the little bungalows which could be bolted shut, it would be impossible for me to get in.

I had really ruined the party for myself. Instead of being able to concentrate on my side of the evening after all the work and effort that I had put in to make it a memorable occasion, all I was concerned with was my predicament.

What in God's name had become of me? I had gone out to Africa for adventure and a challenge, but certainly not of this magnitude. Never had I dreamt that I would own a revolver or possess an uncut diamond that did not belong to me.

On the island that night I was going to be sharing a bungalow with Zola, Pat's personal assistant. At least I had somewhere safe to hide it until I was ready to get rid of it.

Mercifully, I was kept busy all day over on the island, desperately trying not to think about what was ahead of me.

Once or twice Jelani asked me if I was feeling unwell, or if something was troubling me. He knew me so well that it must have been obvious to him that I was not my usual fun self, no matter how much I tried to hide my concern. He was well aware that something was not right. My excuse of being anxious about the party was nonsense as he was aware that I was capable of doing it standing on my head.

There were moments when I came so close to telling him. Just to be able to unburden myself would have been such a relief to me, but it would be so unfair to Jelani as heavens knows what he might do. One thing was for certain though … he would not let Mark get away with it, no matter what it took.

Later in the day, Mark came over with Zola and Harry. Zola had brought a music system from the office which she was to take charge of as they all loved dancing at their parties.

Harry and Mark started erecting the fairy lights through the trees while Jenson was busy starting to slow cook the pig on the spit. Jelani and I lit all the lamps and checked and double checked that every single thing was perfect.

No one, but no one, on this earth would not be impressed as the ambience was wonderful. Almost fictional. The scene was set.

27

All the time I kept thinking how Steve may have handled the situation and what in God's name would he think of me having done nothing to have Mark arrested. There was no doubt that Steve would have confronted Mark and it would all be in the hands of the law. Steve in no way feared for Mark and had nothing to lose. Not like me. It all made me out to be a total bloody coward which I felt ashamed of.

Once I got my bags unpacked in the bungalow, I thought the best place to hide the stone was inside the mattress on my bed. I slit a tiny cut underneath the mattress and slid the stone in. It was to remain there until such times ...

Not that I, in any remote way, feel like getting dressed for a party, but I knew I had to make an effort as it would be expected. I chose to wear my black, silk pants and a beautiful, sequined tunic that I had bought in the Casablanca market. It had been my only indulgence in Morocco.

As I was finishing getting dressed, Zola appeared with two glasses of champagne and saying that Jelani thought I needed a little something. How right he was. Zola looked stunning in a white, short, lace dress which was lovely against her coloured skin. She was a pretty, petite girl with the most wonderful personality. Just the sort of person that lights up a room when she's there.

I pointed out which one was her bed so there was no question about it.

Zola was in a great party mood, as always, and told me that if there was anything I wanted to know about any of the guests she would be able to tell me as her nickname in the office was 'The Walking Encyclopaedia'. She knew everything that went on in Maun, or so she thought!

Pat and David arrived just before their guests started coming over, so we all had time for a drink together and I was able to give them my gift which was eight silver, handcrafted napkin rings. Each had an animal engraved on them and they were truly magnificent. I had them commissioned by a silversmith in Maun so they were a one off. Thankfully, Pat and David were simply lost for words and didn't know how to thank me as they simply adored them, having never seen anything like them before.

As for the way the island looked, it was too much for Pat and she became so emotional with sheer delight. It was all way past their expectations. They had had many parties before, but nothing like this. It was exceptional.

As the guests were arriving, it was Jelani's job to show those with tents where to go. Those in the tents were mostly the younger scene and Pat and David's contemporaries stayed in the bungalows.

The champagne started flowing and the girls were taking round the canapes. Zola had the music started and almost instantaneously the party was in full swing. No time was wasted on introductions and polite getting to know you conversations as everyone knew each other. It was like one big family.

As all my work was done for the party and it was just a case of everyone helping themselves to the food, Pat specified that she wanted me to socialise and enjoy myself. As if I could! But I was prepared to try for their sake and put on a good show.

I was talking to Harry and a cousin of Pat's whom I had met at the office. He was the company accountant and had businesses in Maun and Garabone, and I knew that at some time I could have a tax situation, and may require his services.

It was while we were chatting that over his shoulder I simply could not believe my eyes. Pat was warmly embracing a coloured woman, but to my shock and horror, the man she was with was the same man I had seen with Mallisa and who had met Mark at the airport.

It was imperative to me to find out what the connection was between them and Pat and David. By then I found it impossible to take my eyes off the man whose face I would recognise anywhere.

While I was still trying to hold a conversation with Pat's cousin, I heard Pat calling my name and before I even turned round I just knew who she wanted me to meet.

Just as I thought, she was gesticulating for me to come over and be introduced to her friends. I really would have liked to have found out about them before having to meet him face to face, but I knew there was no way out of it.

When I approached them, Pat put her arm round my shoulder and introduced me as their little jewel of Chiawa, which seemed rather ironic.

Their names were Kyle and Lea Fowrie from Johannesburg who had flown up in their own plane. Most impressive, I thought.

She was so charming and came over as a very gentle and caring person in the short time I was in her company. She did most of the talking, asking me what I thought of Africa and such like. Under different circumstances, she was the kind of woman who would be easy to converse with.

He, on the other hand, hardly said a word except to just stare at me with his extremely menacing face which sent a shiver through my body. It was obvious that, thankfully, he most certainly did not, in any way, recognise me from the Cape.

Pat explained that she and Lea had been friends for many years. They had first been acquainted at an African exhibition where Lea had been exhibiting her bronzes of mostly animals. In fact, as Pat pointed out to me, the handsome bronze sculpture of an elephant and baby in the lodge had been done by Lea.

After a polite length of time, I was able to make an excuse to check the food and disappear. It may just have been my imagination, but I was a little aware of him watching me, or perhaps I was just becoming paranoid.

The whole thing made sense that if Kyle Fowrie was involved in the diamonds, how easy would it be to have Mark pass them on to him, especially with having their own aircraft to take them directly back to Johannesburg. The whole operation could not have been simpler or more foolproof.

What I did find interesting was that throughout the evening, Mark and Kyle Fowrie had nothing to do with each other at all, which made me even more convinced of what was going on as I knew that they were certainly acquainted with one another.

All I prayed for was that the transaction would somehow take place in the morning and not that evening, for my sake.

Mark, mercifully, was running true to form as I watched him steadily get drunker by the minute. Typically, Mark was becoming a nuisance to one of the company pilot's girlfriends. So much so, I wouldn't have been surprised if he got a black eye, which I would have loved to see. Peter, the young pilot, was much stronger looking than Mark and could flatten him in one blow, which would have had most definitely helped me to achieve my task that little bit quicker.

Jenson thought it was the right time to produce the anniversary cake before anymore wine was consumed and the guests were still able to appreciate my work. In all his splendour, Jenson carried it out on a wonderful cake stand to an amazing round of applause with great admiration from everyone. Pat actually felt it was a crime to cut it and wanted to take as many pictures of it before it was demolished!

By that stage, all I wanted was a quiet spell to gather my wits and thoughts so I found a spot under a tree and settled down with a glass of wine. It was no longer than a minute that Zola had spotted me and joined me. It was quite clear to realise that she was a little tipsy in such a funny way and just having a ball to herself.

We chatted about the party and how well it was going. It was obvious how much everyone was enjoying themselves. My feeling was I could ask her about the Fowries without her wondering why, but little did I know it would open the floodgates.

As I had surmised myself, Lea was a truly lovely person who was involved with charity and would do anything for anybody. She had been a very good and kind friend to Pat. However, as for Kyle, no-one liked or trusted him. He treated the staff at the company as if they were below him and hardly conversed at all, apart from with Pat and David.

No one really knew what Kyle's business was, except he was some kind of exporter and importer with involvements in quite a few companies in Africa. He was extremely comfortable and their home outside Johannesburg had to be seen to be believed. He even had a helicopter pad. There was nothing, but nothing, he didn't have.

Lea was a wonderful hostess and was well known for having tennis parties for charity in their beautiful garden, to which she would pay well known tennis players to have a match and she would sell tickets for the charity.

When Pat met Lea at one of her exhibits, Pat and David needed quite a large sum of money to invest in Elite Safaris if they were to expand and keep in competition with all the other new companies that were springing up.

At that time, the bank was being difficult and Pat and David were not at all happy with the interest rates and guarantees they wanted from them. So, it was then that Lea got Kyle interested and within no time, Elite Safaris had the money, plus a silent partner. This really shocked me as, in a way, I was working for this man. It made me feel quite sick at the thought of it. I almost wished Zola hadn't told me.

There was simply no stopping her now as she started on Mark's past, which frankly I was really not interested in. But, nevertheless, I had no option but to listen. She really felt by this time she had a very captivated audience with me.

Seemingly, Mark had been expelled from boarding school in Cape Town. He had been caught selling drugs in school, but the source of the drugs never came to light as he point blank refused to disclose where he had obtained them. His father had many friends and connections, so Mark had no charges brought on him. He was a lucky boy just to be expelled and that would be his only disgrace.

The father managed, through a very close friend who was actually more like an uncle to Mark, to get him a job at a game reserve as the only thing Mark was wonderful with were animals and showed a natural ability with them. He kept himself out of trouble and worked harder than anyone could believe, so within a few years, he was regarded as an excellent warden in the game reserve.

It was while he was working there that he heard of the job of guide at Elite Safaris and managed to impress Pat and David, so he more or less started right away. The clients consider him a first class guide and that is all that is required of him. His personal life never concerned Pat and David.

Zola asked me if I had seen the present that the Fowries had given Pat and David, which I hadn't. The gift had simply stunned Zola. She had never seen anything so magnificent. She described it as the most splendid silver candelabra which would hold three tall candles. At the base there was a figure of a male and female giraffe with baby. It was just so beautiful, but most definitely needed a large dining table which seemingly the Fowries had.

Zola reckoned it cost thousands, but considering what Pat had done for them, it was nothing. By that stage, I was longing to know what she was referring to and Zola was eager to gossip even more.

The one person that her heart went out to was Jelani. She had always thought the world of him. He had been such a loyal, hard worker for the company and he was literally irreplaceable to them. Zola just prayed that he would never find out what happened as it was cruel and he most certainly did not deserve it.

At the time that Leoni had given birth to a girl in Gabarone, where her parents had taken her, it had been a home run by the church where the unmarried gave birth and most of the babies went up for adoption. For some time, Lea had tried to have another child as their first and only child had accidentally drowned in their swimming pool at the age of three. Lea had a nervous breakdown which took a long time to get over as she always blamed herself for taking her eyes off the child she worshipped. When she realised that she was not to have any more children, they tried to adopt through the proper channels, but were turned down because of their ages, although Zola thought there may have been other reasons. It was then that Pat stepped in to help.

She knew Leoni's parents and was well aware that Leoni was not being allowed to keep the baby when it was born so she contacted the parents and the home and put the case forward that it would be far better for the baby to go to such loving and caring people where the child would want for nothing.

Within a short time, a generous donation was given to the home and Leoni's parents received a large amount of money as well. So the Fowrie's became proud parents of a baby boy.

Pat once told Zola that she had accompanied Lea to the home to collect the baby the day after Leoni had given birth. When they arrived, the nurse was already waiting for them, carrying the baby in her arms all wrapped up in a lovely white shawl. As they were leaving with Lea holding her new baby boy, Pat got a glimpse of Leoni standing in a doorway holding a nurse's hand. But it was the look on Leoni's face that would haunt Pat forever. She was so glad Lea did not see her. It was no wonder that Pat and Lea have such a strong bond between them. After all, Pat had managed to give them the greatest gift of all.

The little boy was called Josh and Zola thought he must be about five. She could roughly remember when Pat and David flew down to Johannesburg for his christening as Pat is his godmother.

What really concerned me was how Pat was able to see Jelani so much and know what she had done. Even if some other couple had adopted the baby it would not have been so awful. But this way, some day, Jelani would definitely find out that the Fowries have his son.

I truly felt that if Jelani did know what had happened, then the blame would most definitely be with Mark and knowing how patient and determined a person Jelani is, no matter how long it took he would one day find his revenge.

One thing in Lea's favour was she did not know who the baby's mother was, or her parents, as Pat did all the monetary transactions on her behalf. Nevertheless, in a few years, the Fowries could very possibly take Josh up to Chiawa for a safari and I only hoped and prayed that, by then, Jelani would have moved on in life.

Any spare time that Jelani had, which was not a great deal, he would have his nose stuck in his books. He was studying so hard for a qualification in conservation and wildlife and one day he hoped to apply for a job in Cape Town with the Wildlife Association.

Kerry had been the one to encourage him to do the course as he was aware of how clever and capable Jelani was.

After Jelani left school with a mechanical degree, he got his first job with Elite Safaris looking after the jeeps and planes, but his heart was always in working with animals and that was how he managed to get into the camps as a guide.

I was actually relieved when Zola left to join the others as my mind could not take in anymore. I had heard more than enough gossip for one night to last me a lifetime. I actually wondered if Steve was aware of it all, or would it come as a complete shock to him, too?

I had started to feel I had really had enough. All I wanted was to do what I must and to start afresh with it everything behind me the next day. If only that was possible.

The time was going on and I could see one or two guests starting to go off to bed, although I felt the younger ones may even party all night.

The Fowries said goodnight and retired to their bunga-low which was next to mine.

It wasn't long after that Pat and David made their depar-ture. I had never seen Pat so tipsy and more in need of her bed.

The one person whom I longed to see retire to bed was Mark, but to my dismay, he looked as if he had no intention of doing so, no matter how inebriated he was.

Somehow in my guts, I just felt it was going to be a very long night.

Mark really had never been out my vision all night, even when I was listening to Zola, so I was very confident there had not been a transaction between him and Kyle Fowrie. From what I could see, I didn't even think they had had any conversation at all, which I found very strange.

Jerry was holding court with a few, telling them some of his stories, especially the one about the famous mine in Botswana where the blue diamonds were mined and it had been proven that if they were stolen a curse was then put on the thief. Which was not superstition and that was all I had to hear!

I spotted Zola disappearing into the tent of one of the young guides from another camp in Botswana and I was quite happy as it would make things easier for me if she spent the night with him. At this stage, Mark was starting to make a nuisance of himself with the guests that were left.

From what I was able to see without getting involved, he seemed to have been asking anyone that would listen something to which they all laughed at and told him in no uncertain terms what to do with himself. It was most definitely starting to fire him up as he does not like anyone saying no to him.

Jelani pleaded with me that it was time for me to go to bed as Mark was looking for company to join him on a baby crocodile hunt which Jelani did not want to participate in and wished he may find some way of preventing Mark from this. But to no avail, Mark was more determined than ever and just as Jelani thought, Mark caught sight of me and that was it.

Jelani pleaded with Mark that they should go alone and not involve anyone else, especially as he and most of the guests had had far too much to drink to even contemplate going on such a hunt at that time of night. Needless to say, it was just water off a duck's back to Mark and he was turning rather nasty with Jelani which I would not stand for. So, not knowing what I was letting myself in for, to keep Mark from losing his temper with Jelani and everything turning ugly, I finally agreed to go with them. Very much against my will as the last thing I wanted on earth was to be with Mark on a bloody boat under any circumstances, but especially not that evening.

Mark, as drunk as he seemed, was unfortunately up for anything. He was like a child that did not want the party to end. No wonder everyone that he asked to join him refused to enter into such madness.

I remembered one night, Jerry telling me about the baby crocodile hunt and thinking how dreadful the whole concept of it was. Quite deplorable, in fact. All just for a bit of entertainment.

How anyone may get pleasure out of quietly cruising as near to the river bank holding a lamp over the side of the boat waiting to see the tiny eyes of the baby crocodile, then grabbing it as fast as they could and lifting it on to the boat for those to observe before throwing the poor creature back into the water. If that was entertainment, I had another name for it.

By this stage, Mark was so hyped up it wasn't true. He had a very uncomfortable firm grip on my arm as he walked down to where the boat was. Jelani, by this time, was really looking extremely nervous. It did go through my head that it looked like the few that were still around had now all departed, which meant that no one knew what we were doing.

As it was now getting cold, I asked Mark to let go of my arm so I may go back and fetch a jacket for myself, but at the same time I would try and let Jerry, or someone, know what we were about to do. I just felt that someone should know where we had gone as anything could happen.

Much to my disappointment that was not in Mark's plan as, in so many words, he told me there was no time for such crap.

It had to be the most ridiculous situation that I had ever got myself into in my entire life. I dreaded to think what Steve would say or think when he found out. He would have every right to doubt my sanity as I actually, at that moment, was doing the same.

The smell of alcohol from Mark's breath was disgusting. Heaven knows how much he had drunk. I noticed him stumble a couple of times as we walked, almost knocking me off balance.

Jelani helped me into the boat, just staring at me with the most terrified look in his eyes that I had ever encountered. It certainly did not help the way I was feeling which, by then, was sheer trepidation. My heart was starting to beat so fast that I was terrified of hyperventilating.

Jelani firmly placed me at the very back of the boat and in a way that you would not dare to question. I took it that under no circumstances was I to move from that spot.

Jelani untied the rope and started the engine. Every now and then he would cut it out and we would quietly glide along the side of the grasses and into the slimy green algae.

The only light we had was from the moon and every so often from the huge lamp that Mark was using while hanging over the side of the boat just frantically searching for a pair of tiny eyes which I was inwardly praying he would not find. I thought that it surely could not go on much longer and that he would soon realise he had failed and we could all return to camp.

Every now and then, Mark had this habit of adjusting his belt, purely checking it was still safely on him and it just freaked me out as I knew what it contained.

The night was so still, not even a breeze. The only sounds were from the reeds and bushes scraping against the side of the boat. It was the eeriest thing I had ever heard.

Suddenly, Mark yelled "Yes!" and before I knew it, a little crocodile was aboard screeching horrendously.

Jelani was holding it down behind its head while Mark laughed like a mad man at watching this unfortunate creature wriggling from side to side in sheer desperation to get free. Thankfully, Jelani lifted it and gently lowered it back over the side of the boat into the water.

Never had I sighed such a sigh of relief, knowing we could return and the awful ordeal would be over. But then, I just screamed and screamed at the sight of the most gigantic crocodile emerge from the water and in a second it had Mark by his neck and shoulder with its enormous teeth. In an instant, it swung round and dragged him under the water. My body started to shake from head to toe and I found myself unable to speak a single word, trying desperately to hold my knees as they were jerking out of control.

My brain just could not take in what I had witnessed, as it all happened so fast. There was not one single thing that Jelani or I could have done to save Mark.

As long as I may live, I will never ever be able to erase the vision of Mark being pulled out of the boat in literally the blink of an eye.

Jelani had the lamp over the side shining it on the water, but there was not one solitary piece of evidence that the killing had occurred. Jelani said nothing and wrapped a rug, which had been in the boat, around me as my body temperature was dropping rapidly. I had never felt so cold in my life and I was finding it very difficult to even think straight, let alone talk.

When we arrived back at the island, everyone had gone to bed and I didn't know if I was relieved or not. There was still some heat from the fire, but Jelani threw on a couple of logs and literally placed me down beside the heat. He then brought me a mug of sweet tea, although I felt more like a bottle of cognac.

It had to be the most surreal situation that anyone could imagine themselves encountering. I kept praying that I would wake and find it was all just a horrific nightmare, but to no avail.

Mercifully by now, my body stopped shaking and I could feel my blood getting warmer, although I still found it difficult to get the right words out.

So much was going through my mind of what was going to happen. One thing was for certain, I knew as long as I lived, I would never ever be able to forget what occurred. From that moment on, every time I closed my eyes, I would see the jaws of the crocodile open, the teeth crushing down on Mark and the sound of bones snapping like brittle twigs.

Jelani came and sat down beside me and almost at the same time, we both looked over towards Mark's tent which I couldn't believe he would never return to. Soon, it was going to be morning and everyone would drift off, but before all of that, Jelani wanted me to listen to him very carefully.

The fact was, Mark was gone and nothing on this earth would ever bring him back. There would never be a body for the police or anyone else to find. So Mark and the diamonds had disappeared for an eternity.

Jelani quietly explained to me that Mark had been smuggling diamonds out of South Africa for some time and was certain that Kyle Fowrie was his accomplice to whom he handed them over to. Jelani had known of Mark's dealings for many years from an informant who had worked in the mines.

Jelani was also convinced that there was a possibility

that Mark would have had the diamonds on his person when he was taken by the croc, as there was no way that he would leave them at any time in his tent.

Jelani assured me that the people Mark was involved with would stop at nothing to find the diamonds, and with their way of thinking of not ever trusting a living sole, to them it was possible that we knew of the diamonds and had killed Mark, which most definitely gave cause to fear for our lives.

Our safest way was for Mark to have simply vanished that night into thin air, with us knowing absolutely nothing of his disappearance.

The Botswana police would be notified of his disappearance and would search the island. They would, of course, find nothing at all, so at the end of it, they would most probably come up with the explanation that he met with a tragic accident, death by misadventure and no more police time would be wasted on him, unlike his partners in crime who would not let it go and would continue to search for Mark and their diamonds, no matter how long it would take.

I was so close to telling Jelani that I actually had a diamond, but that would put his life in jeopardy as well as mine already was.

Knowing now there was no way on earth I could disclose any of this to Steve and risk endangering his life, it was my burden forever and I would have to carry it alone.

I sat in my bungalow until dawn, thinking what in God's name would I do about the stone. I knew my only safe option was to keep it until Mark's disappearance off the face of the earth was forgotten about, or at least until the cartel accepted the fact they had lost their diamonds forever.

I knew that once everyone had left, I would have a chance to look in Mark's tent to see if I may find any kind of information regarding his contacts, especially on Kyle Fowrie for a start.

Once Jelani got back to Chiawa, he was firstly going to contact Pat and David, who by then would be in Maun and it would be their responsibility to alert the Botswana police.

Jelani and I knew that someone would have to stay on the island until the police came, which would most certainly be within a few hours and as I was in the charge of the party, they most definitely would want to talk to me.

Our story was simple in that everyone went to bed and left Mark drinking on his own, which was not unusual at all.

As far as the rest of the guests, they all had so much alcohol that not one of them was capable of remembering who or what they saw that night.

Jelani assured me it would be an open and shut case and there was not one piece of evidence to in any way associate us with the disappearance of Mark.

He had checked the boat in daylight and there wasn't even a scratch where the crocodile had come over, not even one spot of blood. How extraordinary that something so monstrous could happen and leave no trace at all.

It was amazing how everyone departed without a question of not seeing Mark for breakfast, even Pat and David must have just assumed he was still out for the count.

The one and only person that made a remark was Kyle Fowrie to his wife in that he was seeing Mark next week in Johannesburg for a meeting and did not have time to wait until he surfaced from a drunken sleep as time was of the essence for him to fly back to Johannesburg that morning. I was never so damn relieved to hear those words uttered from his mouth.

Jelani promised me that once he informed the police, he would come back to the island so that I would not be left alone to face the questioning. Once the police had been notified of Mark being missing, they asked questions at Elite Safaris to those who had been at the party and thankfully they all had the same story of Mark drinking heavily and no one had any idea of when he went to his tent.

I knew that Jelani would be back shortly, so if I was looking in Mark's tent it had to be now. By this time, I was beginning to become quite amazed at myself as the thought of Mark having gone off this earth forever did not really disturb me. In a strange way, it was a relief in that he was no longer any kind of threat to my relationship with Steve.

It was certainly a strange feeling when entering Mark's tent. His black leather jacket was lying on the camp bed beside a couple of books and in the corner sat his large green canvas travel bag. In the bag he had a bottle of whisky and his toiletries, plus other bits and pieces. But it was the little black Filofax tucked under his sweater that I was more interested in. I sat on the bed and started going through it page after page.

It literally consisted of dozens of names and addresses. I recognised some of them, especially Mary-Louise and her mother's address in America. Not only the home address, but phone number as well. At the bottom of one of the places in very small print was a name, Franz, and underneath an address I presumed, 'Hoveniersstraat 9. Amsterdam'. There was no doubt in my mind what that was for.

Very carefully, I removed that page and slid it in my pocket. There was nothing else of any great consequence in his bag, so I left his tent and waited for Jelani and the police to arrive.

When the police arrived on the island, absolutely every single thing that Jelani said would happen did happen. I couldn't believe how calm and assured of myself that I had become, after all, I had nothing to be anxious of in their minds.

The whole process only took a couple of hours while they searched the island and his tent and came up with not one solitary clue as to what may have happened. The police sergeant, who knew Jelani, just seemed to accept that Mark had wandered off in a drunken state and met his fate, i.e. drowning.

Mark had been involved with the local police a couple of times regarding minor car incidents involving drink, and was noted by them as being an extremely foolish young man who one day would come a cropper.

That day, I went back to Chiawa to prepare for our next group of clients. It all just seemed like business as usual and

Mark would soon be history for everyone, he had no family and very few friends that would give him much thought. As for Kyle Fowrie, he would have some explanations to the diamond cartel and he better hope they believed him.

Ironically enough, it would be I that would not forget him as long as I possessed the stone, which I now felt was mine.

My long term plan was when I was finished with Elite Safaris and Steve and I were married that we would make a visit to Europe and have a few days in Amsterdam. While Steve did the tourist trail, I would take a business trip to Hoveniersstrat 9, and then would, hopefully, be able to make a handsome investment for Steve and myself which would secure our future, and Steve would be told the money was an unexpected inheritance from an old aunt.

After all, how many of us walks this earth without 'a little secret'?

28

Working in the camp was now never going to be quite the same for me, with so many memories that frankly I would love to forget.

It was the strangest thing that no one ever mentioned Mark's name, almost as if he had never existed. I even felt that I would never talk of him to Jelani, in fact it felt as if it were a taboo subject.

The great love that I had Chiawa was not the same, I felt that not only did it change my life in so many ways and, latterly, certainly not for the better as it left a life lasting memory that would be impossible to erase.

As the months went by, it became very obvious to Steve that my feelings and enthusiasm for my job were definitely not the same, something had changed which concerned him and he was constantly enquiring if there was any kind of problem with Elite Safaris that he could sort out for me.

Luckily, he accepted the fact that I was in need of a new challenge and missed him so desperately the weeks we were apart, which was the truth.

We both made the decision for me to leave Elite Safaris and for us to get married as soon as possible.

Pat and David were utterly gutted and tried in many ways to tempt me to stay, but as they knew it was not the sort of business to be in if your heart and soul were no longer in it. I promised that I would stay until someone was able to replace me, which Pat and David were well aware would be a hard task.

It did take some time before a couple from Zimbabwe were appointed, they had been running their own small hotel and for years had been longing to find the right move for them as everything had become such a struggle financially.

It was agreed that what had happened when I joined the company was that I would be staying a week with them, I just hoped and prayed that Jelani would like them and would be happy to work with them. My only big regret was that I was leaving him, we had formed such a bond that I could not bear to think that we may lose touch.

Wendy and Bill Montford arrived in Chiawa and from the very beginning I took an instant liking to them both. They were not afraid of hard work and Bill was a first class chef, not quite so fine dining as mine, but he produced good food, certainly up to standard for the guests.

It was heart-warming for me to see Jelani liking them so much. On my part, I could not have given them a more glowing reference on Jelani, and told them how important it was to have him. For me, it was a great comfort as there was no doubt that I was leaving Chiawa in capable hands and would look forward to coming back with Steve as clients one day.

I did wonder how I would feel once I had left and hoped to hell that I had made the right decision.

We had a small party in camp the night before I left

which was rather emotional with the girls singing to me and Jenson and Jelani saying that I had been the best thing that had happened to Chiawa.

In the morning, Jelani drove me to the airstrip for the Cessna to take me to Maun. My heart was heavy with such mixed emotions, there would always be a little part of me left in Chiawa.

Jelani said not one word on the journey to me and I knew how he felt as it was so difficult to put into words.

The plane was waiting for me and as I took my bags from Jelani to say goodbye, he just looked at me with his enormous brown eyes as tears gently rolled down his cheeks. I hugged him and just held him tight for a moment, but found it impossible to say anything.

Once on board and in the air looking down on every-thing that I loved and had become such a way of life, my tears flowed nearly all the way to Maun.

When we touched down, I could see Steve standing and from that moment, all my fears disappeared and I realised, yet again, another chapter of my life was about to start.

29

Steve had been incredible, he had almost organised the whole wedding from caterers to a huge marquee, he even had an appointment made for us to see the local minister who was to marry us in the garden of his home.

All that was left for me to do was to see to my wedding dress which I was going to buy from a bridal boutique in Jo'Burg, and luckily, I knew exactly what I wanted, I just hoped they would have it. Steve and I flew down to Jo'Burg and met the family friend who had the jewellers.

For me, it was a strange experience looking at all the beautiful diamond rings realising how these stones looked before being cut, apart from being aghast at the cost of them, God knows the value of my stone.

The last ring I wanted was a solitaire diamond which, unfortunately, Steve was keen for me to have.

The ring that I could not take my eyes off was a square cut emerald in a modern setting, it was a fraction too large, but Mr Levy would be able to get the alteration done while he and Steve went for lunch, to leave me to attend to my dress search.

There was a bridal boutique in the mall which I had spotted the last time in Jo'Burg, but wedding dresses had been the last thing on my mind.

There were only two dresses that I knew would be me, and the second one was all I had ever dreamed about, so simple, but just beautiful. It was ivory ribbon lace, strapless, but had a shrug that I could take off in the evening, the skirt flowed softly over my body to my ankles, perfect for dancing and showing off some stylish wedding shoes which I bought there and then.

Steve and I met back at the jewellers to collect my ring and he was amazed how quickly I had been able to purchase everything I needed.

That evening, we flew back to Maun with our wonderful purchases. On board, Steve ordered two glasses of champagne and, as the stewardess brought them, he placed a tiny box on my tray, I realised it was not my ring as it was securely placed on my finger which I could not stop looking at and felt unbelievably lucky.

Inside the box was a pair of diamond earrings. I could not believe my eyes as they were stunning. Never in my life had I ever owned such exquisite jewellery.

This was his wedding gift to me which made me think what on earth was I to buy him.

The wedding was a tremendous success, with mother and George flying out from the UK. They had been in South Africa prior to the wedding and had taken the Blue Train from Cape Town up to Jo'Burg and then flew into Maun.

There was no doubt that our wedding was the most memorable and the best day of my life.

Steve's sister had organised all the flowers right down to my pretty cream rose posy.

On the large lawn they had erected a canopy decorated with amazing flowers, this was where we took our vows.

There was also a path of rose petals from the house to where Steve stood waiting for me. As I entered the garden, an African choir started to sing. I don't think there was a dry eye amongst our guests, including Steve, who was so emotional that I really realised just how much he loved me. I had to be the luckiest girl alive to have been given this chance of a wonderful future with someone like Steve.

After we were married, Steve and I had a week in the Seychelles while mother and George went on a safari to one of Elite Safaris camps. Mother felt she did not want to go to Chiawa if I was not to be there, it just did not feel right, actually it was how I felt as well.

On our return from our honeymoon, Mary, who was Steve's housekeeper, whom I had become so fond of had prepared a wonderful, welcoming dinner. There was nothing that she would not do for me and I knew how valuable she would be when I started working in my own restaurant and especially, God willing, the day would come when we had a family.

Mary had been with his parents since she was very young and had looked after Steve when he was just a little boy. There was a little house in the grounds where Mary lived alone as she had never married, so totally devoted was she to the Prentice family.

There was something about her that reminded me of Jelani, the same smile and committed loyalty to whoever she worked for. Her energy was amazing, she seemed to work all day with never a complaint, singing in the most pleasing voice. I could imagine her lullaby would send any baby to sleep.

The amount of wedding gifts was almost embarrassing. We even received lovely gifts from people who had not been at the wedding.

Although Steve did not need a single thing for the house as he had inherited not only the house, but all contents – whereas his sister was left a sum of money which suited her best – it was a joy for us to have these gifts to call our own, no matter how much we appreciated his parents valuables.

One or two boxes had arrived when we were in the Seychelles. Steve and I were like kids at Christmas opening them with each one delighting us as more and more from kitchenware, table linen and china, even a few cheques.

There was one fairly large box that had been delivered by Fedex from Jo'burg stamped all over it with 'Fragile – handle with care'. Eventually, after getting off all the tape, we finally got it open.

After emptying masses of polystyrene it revealed a beautiful gift-wrapped box with cream ribbons. Steve lifted the box carefully out of the container and handed me the gift card.

Neither of us had any idea who this may be from, and on opening and reading it I tried so hard not to show the shock on my face as there had to be some explanation to this. Thankfully, Steve did not see my reaction as he was too busy unwrapping very elegant crystal champagne flutes, they must have cost a great deal of money. Steve was so delighted with them as his parents had nothing like them, they really were stunning.

I passed the card to him and quietly asked why Kyle and

Lea Fowrie would send us a wedding gift. I had no idea that he even knew them as he never once mentioned their names to me and had not even been on the invitation list.

This was so horrendous for me, as I could not divulge to Steve my reasons for my great concern and hated myself for not being able to tell him. He was such an honest person. How would he feel that his wife had a stolen diamond. I was not prepared to take the chance; he might be appalled at me and perhaps look at me in a totally different light. I made the mistake and will have to live with it.

Fortunately, Steve was rather surprised on why we had received such a handsome present. He had only met Kyle Fowrie a few times when his father was alive as sometimes Steve would accompany his father to Jo'burg to buy ceramics and such like for their garden centre, as Fowrie had the largest company selling them. In fact, it was through Kyle Fowrie that Steve's father met and became friends with Victor Levy, the jeweller from where my engagement ring and earrings came from.

I had thought that Mr. Levy was a delightful old man and had felt sorry for him when he told us he had no family to take on the business and would have to just keep going until he had enough, but not to worry, as he had already had a marvellous offer from a friend. There is no wondering who the damn friend was. How convenient that acquisition would be, the world would be his oyster being able to cut and sell the stones under his own roof.

Steve and I came to the conclusion that the Fowrie's must have heard of our marriage through Pat and David as I had only met them once at the silver wedding party. This gift was purely because of Steve's father.

I had most definitely become paranoid in wondering if Kyle had any idea that Jelani and I had anything to do with Mark's disappearance and the diamonds, after all, we must have been the last people to see him alive.

If Kyle was the middleman in the transactions, he would most certainly be answerable to some undesirables to say the least. It would take a lot for them to believe that Mark disappeared into thin air with their fortune.

It was obvious to me that I could not rest and put all this out of mind, once and for all, until the diamond was out of my possession. Only then, God willing, I might have peace of mind and get on with this wonderful life that Steve had created for me.

My first project was to sell my little house, but that came as no problem as a doctor who worked in the hospital had, for some time, been looking for the right property and had heard, through the grapevine, that I may be selling.

Dr Samatry bought my house at nearly double the price I had paid. It was simply amazing; no advertising or such like It could not have been easier, he even bought the soft furnishings and patio furniture, including the BBQ, as he loved to entertain.

He was quite young and had been a Doctor in Gaborone when he got the chance of gaining a lot more money in running an Aids clinic in Maun. He seemed a kind and gentle guy who I felt happy to have my house and that he would be so happy living there. He even asked if Steve and I, once we were settled, would come over to him for a few drinks. It is strange how, in the most unlikely circumstances, you can meet someone and straight away wish to become friends and feel that they are truly trustworthy. Steve felt exactly the same, in fact, he stated that it was no bad thing to have a friend or contact in the local hospital as you never knew when you might need it.

30

There were a few changes that Steve and I wanted to do to the interior of the family house as it had been neglected a little and needed some TLC.

Our main project was to blitz the kitchen which I had great ideas for, wanting to make it as open plan as possible, especially with me being the one spending most of the time in it. Although Steve could cook, it was purely out of necessity and he just relished the thought of the good food I was going to produce for him through our married life.

We had been settled in sometime when Pat came to see me with an offer.

The company wished me to prepare certain dishes that would be flown fresh to the camps, especially my extraordinary canapes and some that could be frozen; all of this would be simply effortless for me, especially when the kitchen had been modernised.

The idea of it really appealed to me, here was something I could do in my home at my leisure until I felt like starting a restaurant in Maun which Steve was not so happy about, as he thought it would take up too much time away from him which I suppose was correct, this was why Pat's proposal was ideal as we could still have plenty of quality time together.

Pat agreed that once the kitchen was up and running in a couple of months, only then would I start, and that it would be entirely up to me the quantities that I would be preparing for them. I would bill them monthly and would receive immediate payment to our bank account in Maun.

Steve was so impressed how professional and business-like I was as he had never seen this side of me before, but I was determined that all of this would be on my terms, or not at all. The transportation and refrigeration of the food had to be up to my standard as if anything was not right, I would take no blame knowing that when the food was delivered to them it will be in perfect condition.

I would not be employed by Elite Safaris as previous, but purely an independent supplier providing a service which I was free to terminate at any time.

Steve was convinced that once word got out in Maun that I was doing home catering that orders would come flying in from other sources and perhaps, in the future, may actually require premises in Maun if all of this really took off, but one step at a time, he had such great expectations of me which was so flattering.

Steve had been absolutely correct, once I started catering for Elite Safaris it was amazing how many orders I was receiving from people. I had no idea so much entertaining took place in Maun. Through Mary, I was able to employ one of her friends who was looking for a small job as Mary and I were definitely requiring another pair of hands in the kitchen.

Maun is such a small town that everyone just about knows everything about each other. It turned out that my new help, Belita, was, in fact, a cousin of Leoni's mother who was well aware of what happened to Jelani's child, she also informed me that Leoni was working in Durban as a nanny for a couple who had a law firm.

I was quite surprised how much information Belita had. She felt that Jelani was well aware of what had happened to his and Leoni's baby and when the time was right, he would find Leoni and start a life together. How I wished this would be true. If anyone deserved a chance in life, it was Jelani.

Belita was a wonderful character; she never stopped talking, laughing and singing while she worked, she must have been the happiest person ever, her clothes were just like her demeanour, so colourful. She certainly did not hide her size, in fact she was very proud of being a big girl. There was something motherly about her that I loved. The three of us made such a good team it could not have been better.

The girls had been aware that I was feeling more tired than usual and had become a bit picky with my food, and had most definitely gone off my sundowner: a glass of chilled Chablis at night with Steve after he finished work. I thought a visit to my doctor might be a good idea in case I required some vitamins, or such like.

The morning I was due to go, Belita came to me and gave me one of her big hugs and declared that I was wasting my time going to the doctor as she knew what was up with me.

Laughingly I told her that she did not know everything and she was no doctor, to which she replied that you don't have to be a doctor to know when someone is pregnant.

It was obvious, seemingly, to her, I had a look that she had seen many times before.

I really wasn't amazed at this, as it had crossed my mind, perhaps by the grace of God, that this might be the case, but hadn't wanted to dwell on it just in case all I needed were some vitamins.

There was no way I was going to mention my thoughts to Steve for fear of disappointing him in case I was not expecting our baby, as I knew how desperate he was to start a family.

When I arrived back from the doctors, Belita had finished her work and had left for home, but faithful little Mary was waiting in the garden for me with a tray of tea and cookies. She just knew by the huge smile on my face, without even telling her, that Belita had been quite right: I was indeed pregnant.

We sat and chatted and planned while drinking tea under the mashatu tree for shade, she was so excited and happy for us and without even being asked, she would be taking on the job of nanny, there was utterly no question that she would not. I was totally euphoric and could hardly contain myself until Steve got home.

The first thing Steve did on coming home was to kiss me then quickly get showered and changed, we would get together on the patio for our sundowners and catch up on our day.

Sometimes we would have two large gin and tonics, or a glass of wine, but tonight, I had poured Steve a glass of bubbly and had a small bottle of sparkling water for myself.

There was a look of bewilderment on his face at the drinks, then he took one look at my face which was nearly bursting with joy and he just screamed, 'You are having a baby.' Steve held me in his arms and I could feel the tears from him on my cheeks.

We were both just encapsulated in sheer happiness, there was so much to talk about. I really had to try and calm him down as the first thing that we had to do was call my mother and his sister and give them the wonderful news which we knew would delight them both so much.

We decided which one of our bedrooms would be turned into a nursery, obviously the one nearest us. As Steve was very good with his hands, he was going to make the cot and some pretty furniture as well.

The baby was going to be born in the early spring, which was perfect timing as it wasn't too hot and the baby and I would be able to spend time in the garden.

Life could not get any better. For the first time, I felt so complete and secure, but there was only one thing that I had to do before this innocent little baby came into the world and that was to rid myself of the diamond once and for all, only then would it be possible to erase the past.

It was most certainly a week of great news as my friend Jerry handed in a letter from Jelani which he had brought down from Chiawa.

At last Jelani had passed his exams and was so excited the W.W.F in Cape Town were to give him an interview with a possible job involving him in a rhino project which would be simply perfect for him. With his amazing tracking expertise, he would be so valuable to them. Indeed, this was most certainly the right time for Jelani and I to move on with our lives.

In his letter he expressed how Jensen and everyone

agreed that when I had left Chiawa the heart of it had gone, as I had brought something very special to the camp that had never been there before. Even as good as Wendy and Bill Montford were to work for, the magic had disappeared so nothing would be the same.

Jensen was going to retire once Jelani had left which would be a total change over at Chiawa, not that the clients would know the difference, but I am sure Pat and David may sense the camp lacked that special charm that we all gave it as being one happy family which was unique.

Luckily, I was able to convince Steve that it was a good idea before I became too pregnant for us to have a short holiday: one place I had never been to was Amsterdam and I would love to see it.

Steve, bless him, as usual, was more than happy to go along with my plan, the only place in Europe he had been to was London with his father and mother when he was a young boy, other than that his life had been in Africa.

The best deal in flights for us was to fly to Gabarone then one stop with Air Kenya to Jo'burg then on to Amsterdam. Mary and Belita were now more than capable of looking after the catering side of everything for the short time we were to be away. All they had to do was to keep to my plan and follow the instructions and nothing could go wrong.

Mary had a good brain in her and was much brighter than Belita who tended to panic if she was not sure of something, that's why Mary always kept a watchful eye on her.

31

We landed in Schiphol Airport in the evening, so later, all we had to do was to find our hotel, have some dinner and chill out as I was very tired from the journey.

The Hotel Mosaic was ideal, right in the centre of the city and so near to all the tourist attractions for us.

We were so spoilt for choice of restaurants, but decided on a small bistro near our hotel which luckily had wonderful food, then opted for an early night.

I spent a couple of days with Steve going to the Rijksmuseum and seeing works by Rembrandt and such like, it was amazing to see it all.

Amsterdam was everything it was made out to be, we loved all it had to offer, there was almost too much to see and do in only a short stay.

It was the second to last day that I decided to sell the stone and be done with it. How lucky had I been that the stone had never been detected through any of the security checks? I had wrapped it in cotton wool then put that deep inside a large jar of body cream and managed to reseal the jar which was inside my toilet bag in my case; so incredible how it must have been truly masked. As Steve hated shopping, he was more than happy to do more sightseeing, especially the canals, and leave me to baby shop. We had arranged that our rendezvous would be in Vondelpark at the Vertigo Restaurant for lunch.

This left me just the morning to do what I came to achieve, so there was no time to waste. Once I was out of his sight, I hailed a taxi to take me to *Hovenierstraat 9*.

The whole time I was in the taxi, I felt my stomach starting to churn over with nerves and yet again my hands were sweating, surely this behaviour was not good for my baby, but like it or not, I had to get on with it. The moment had arrived.I had spent many sleepless nights wondering how it would go, and now here it was at last.

The taxi stopped outside a row of high flats in the old part of Amsterdam; such a narrow street, no wonder it was one way. I had tried to pay attention to where I was going so when I came out I had a rough idea where I was, as most certainly did not have time to get lost.

Once I climbed a few steps up to a dark green door there was a plaque on the wall with quite a few names. On searching down through the names, second to last was the name Franz Bessinck. My heart was now thumping no matter how much I tried deep breathing. Could I really go through with this? Should I take the easy way out and simply drop the damn thing in a canal and clear my conscience once and for all? No, I had come too far to do that. Knowing that once I entered the building there was no going back, did I really have the nerve to go ahead with my plan now it was reality?

It was as if I was being led by some force inside me. I opened the door and found myself standing in a long, dark hallway. On one side of the hall it had numerous bicycles up against it which were all chained up, on the other side there was another plate with even more names than had been outside, but there was his, fifth floor which was the top.

Thankfully, I could see a lift at the end of the hall. It had a huge iron gate to open, but inside was so claustrophobic, certainly only room for one more and that may be at a squeeze. The lift rattled and jolted and seemed to take forever to reach the top floor. When it finally came to a halt the gate was opened for me by a tall, grey-haired man, extremely elegant in a pinestriped suit with a bright red tie. He smiled and bowed his head to me as I came out of the lift and gave me such a charming good morning, it did cross my mind if this was my Franz Bessinck and I had missed him.

On the landing there were three doors. I could see one was accountants and another a doctor of psychiatry: the way I was feeling that should have been the one to enter. I rang the bell on Franz Bessinck's door and for what seemed like ages, it was finally opened by a very pretty young girl. I asked if I could see Franz Benninck. She led me into a small hallway and asked my name, which I made up on the spot, how stupid I had been not to think of a name before going so far. For some bazar reason, Anne Bell just flew out of my mouth with no connection to anyone or anything. She disappeared and after a few minutes led me along the corridor and into a small room.

Behind an enormous desk, a small, grey-bearded man stood up and shook my hand. He stared at me through little spectacles which were on the end of his nose.

He must have been a fair age, but there was something kindly about him that put me at ease a little.

He pointed to the chair for me to sit down and asked in perfect English if his granddaughter might bring me some coffee. Franz sat back in his chair with his arms crossed, obviously waiting for me to speak first. With one deep breath, I explained that I wished to sell a stone and would he be interested.

He said nothing, which I found really disconcerting and just sat and watched while I fumbled in my bag and brought out the stone which I placed in front of him.

By now, I needed water more than coffee, or anything, as my mouth had become so parched my tongue felt like cotton wool. He picked up the stone and put what resembled a magnifying glass to his eye to look at it closely. After a long examination, he got up and placed it on some very fancy looking scales.

His granddaughter brought in the coffee and I was able to ask for some water, thank god.

The silence was killing me, but I felt it was best to try and look confident. This had to be the hardest act I ever had to do.

All I was praying for was I would not be asked how much I wanted for the stone if he was prepared to buy, as I did not have a clue and could totally blow how ignorant I was in this matter. There was no doubt that Franz Bessinck was well aware how much I was out of my comfort zone, this was a very shrewd little man who had probably seen the likes of me before.

There was still no conversation and I, for one, was not, or could not, even try to enter into small talk even to break the awkward silence; also, there was no expression on his face as to what he thought of the stone, he just got up and walked to the corner of his office. It was then I noticed he had a limp and seemed to drag his foot, he was much older than I had first thought he was.

There was a large safe, where, with his back to me, I could hear the bleep of a code being put in, then with a slow buzz came a loud click.

While I waited with bated breath, I looked around the room where I noticed two cameras, one in each corner with a little red light flashing.

He came back and sat down with a grey envelope which he simply slid over the desk to me.

With one of his strange smiles he stated that there was two hundred thousand euros in the envelope and he would quite understand if I wished to count it before I left and that he would not be offended. To sit in his office in front of him and count this money was the last thing possible, for a start my hands were shaking and all I wanted was out of there and into the fresh air.

I had no idea how much the stone had been worth, but this was so much more than I ever dreamed of, I was truly flabbergasted. Franz Bessinck stood up and shook my hand calling for his granddaughter to show me out.

As I left his office, I did manage to turn round and simply say thank you. In fact, during the whole episode I had hardly spoken at all to him.

Outside in the corridor was the lift, but I could not face that again, so I took the stairs instead, as they were my only option. Descending the stairs seemed to take forever, but finally I made it to the bottom and in no time I was out in the fresh air.

It was such a beautiful day with a clear blue sky and crisp air; the sort of day that makes you feel so lucky to be alive. I felt like a massive weight had been lifted off my shoulders; so much so, that I just wanted a good cry, as it would feel like a release valve.

Within a couple of blocks, I was in the city square where I saw the Bank of Switzerland. The bank was very majestic inside, with huge marble pillars and a very ornate ceiling with a splendid chandelier hanging from it. There was a great feeling of grandeur there.

Thankfully, there were not many people in the bank waiting for service, but what was very evident were the two armed guards walking round slowly, observing everything and everyone. I walked straight up to the teller who was behind a large glass partition and informed him I would like to make a deposit and open an account.

It was incredible how easy it all was. He asked for my name and passport then handed me a form to sign, the money was then given to him, which he slowly counted, at least twice; yes indeed, two hundred thousand euros to the penny.

Within minutes, a small red deposit book with my name, account number and transaction was printed out, he also gave me literature on the bank then wished me good day.

It was done and dusted and I still had time to shop before meeting Steve. Totally incredible what I had managed to achieve in just one morning, not a bad day's business, I thought. A little retail therapy was what I needed to calm myself; there was a fabulous baby and maternity shop close by where I managed to do quite a bit of damage to my credit card.

Everything that I had purchased for our baby was in white or lemon as we did not want to know if it was a boy or a girl before birth. They had some rather stylish maternity wear that I could not resist and knew I would not see in Maun.

It had been so wonderful if only I could have told Steve about our new account, but was well aware that it would come to him one day as a surprise, or sooner if I thought he would understand my motives and not chastise me forever.

As I entered the Vertigo Restaurant in the park, I could see Steve sitting at a table with a beer and reading some sort of map. My heart just filled with sheer joy at the sight of him, he really had become the most important person in my life, I could never ever dream of being without him as he brought love and utter happiness into my life that I did not imagine was possible.

That evening, as it was our last in Amsterdam, we had dinner at the most wonderful Michelin star restaurant called Vinkeles, just the type of restaurant that once I would have owned, there was not one thing that was not utter perfection from food to ambience. This was the right place for a celebration which I was certainly doing, even if I had to keep it to myself.

Steve remarked how much better I was looking compared to this morning, that awful strained look had left me and I was back as radiant as ever. If he knew what I had been through, I doubt that he would actually believe me and I would not blame him as it was hard for me to believe it as there was something fanciful about it.

Next morning, we arrived at Schiphol Airport to embark on our long journey home. I was so eager to leave and head for Africa with only our new baby to think about.

Once airborne, the steward handed round the daily papers and Steve was so pleased that he managed to get his favourite which was the *Cape Times*; there was always interesting articles that caught his attention.

He was halfway through the paper while, in the meantime, I had settled into my book feeling so relaxed it wasn't true. He passed the *Times* to me and pointed to a headline that he thought may just interest me.

'Diamonds are forever, but not for this old croc'

A crocodile in the Delta had tried to attack tourists in a boat, so was shot and killed, and as this was unusual for this type of attack it was assumed the croc must have been ill so an autopsy took place, which divulged human remains plus a quantity of uncut diamonds and parts of a watch that had not yet eroded with initials that were still legible of MC, which the Botswana police said had belonged to Mark Compton who had disappeared some time ago. The diamonds were now the property of the Botswana Government and the missing persons case on Mark Compton was now closed.